September, 2005

To Nicholas,

with best wishes,

Eleanor Rosellini

Other books by the author

The Puzzle in the Portrait
(2003-2004 Young Hoosier Book Award Finalist)

The Mystery
of the
Ancient Coins

Eleanor Florence Rosellini

Illustrations by Jennifer P. Goldfinger

Guild Press Emmis Books

GUILD PRESS EMMIS BOOKS
10665 Andrade Drive
Zionsville, Indiana 46077
1-800-913-9563
www.guildpress.com

ISBN: 1-57860-125-8

Library of Congress
Catalog Card Number
2001012345

Printed and bound in the United States of America

Dedicated to the memory of my mother,
Marguerite Zimmermann Florence,
and to all who enliven the world with humor and joy.

The Mystery Letter

"Jonathan, you are so disgusting!" Elizabeth Pollack, ace detective, stood in her grandfather's living room on a snow-covered December morning. She glared at her younger brother, whose nose was deeply buried in a box of chocolates. Jonathan blissfully sniffed his way down the first row of candies, like a bee flitting from flower to flower.

"Get your nose out of there, Jon. You're slobbering all over the candy."

"I'm not slobbering." Jonathan straightened up to his full height—a skinny four feet, three inches. "You said I'm supposed to practice being a detective. So I'm training my nose. I can tell if a piece has vanilla or raspberry filling, just by smelling. Then I dig a hole in the bottom and see if I'm right. Great, huh?" Jonathan hung his chunky front teeth over his lower lip and rolled his eyeballs back. It was his latest trick. Goof smile with zombie eyes. He snapped his face back to normal as he popped a chocolate into his mouth. "But I wish Pop would get some chocolate-covered grasshoppers. They're even better, 'cause they're nice and crunchy."

Elizabeth didn't give Jonathan the pleasure of a grimace. He was the kind of eight-year-old brother who lived only to annoy. "You must be crazy, messing around with Pop's candy," she said. "You know he'll find out." Their grandfather, Pop, noticed everything. Way down deep, he was nice, but mostly he went through life at a low grumble. "And anyway, Jonathan, I don't think you even care about being a detective."

"Yeah? Well, if you're Miss Perfect Detective, how come you can't find that letter Pop lost?"

Elizabeth felt herself stiffen. The missing letter. It was the best—and worst—thing that had happened in months. A week before Christmas, their grandfather had received a letter in his post office box. It wasn't written to him, but instead was mysteriously addressed to *Detectives Elizabeth and Jonathan Pollack.* Pop put it in a safe place, so they would find it when they arrived for their visit. But by the time they came, Pop had forgotten where the safe place was. They searched everywhere, all the rooms, upstairs and down, and every piece of prim old furniture. Two days of hunting, and the letter was still missing.

"I just hope Pop didn't throw it away by mistake," Elizabeth said. "Things are always disappearing around here." She had never met anyone more fiercely neat than her grandfather. Pop was beyond tidy. He was at war with clutter, and his stormy clean-ups usually meant trouble. Christmas money would disappear, crumpled up with used gift wrap. Rings would be flung into the garbage, mistaken for pop-up tops from soda cans.

"Well, I don't think Pop threw it away," said Jonathan. "I bet that letter is right in this room." He peeked behind the wooden legs of a stiff, leather sofa, then shuffled through a pile of travel magazines on the coffee table.

"I don't know. It seems like we've looked everywhere." Elizabeth stared out the picture window, but she found nothing to cheer her up. The world looked as if it had been washed with a dirty rag. At the bottom of the hill the lake lay flat and dull under a sulky gray sky. Even the snow had lost its sparkle. Christmas Day had been different—full of sunshine and bright as a brass band. The house had been happy, too, almost like when Gran was alive. But then it was time for everyone to go home. Their aunt and cousins left first. Their father went back to Indiana to a teachers' meeting. Elizabeth and Jonathan stayed behind with their mother to spend a few extra days with Pop. Elizabeth didn't mind staying—except for the quiet. It drifted in as soon as the others were gone, spreading stillness through the house like a fine layer of dust.

"Okay, let's get going, Jon. Mom said we're supposed to have this place cleaned up before they get back from the store."

"I *am* cleaning up." Jonathan grabbed a wadded-up ball of gift wrap and raced twice around the coffee table. "And he dodges. He fakes. Two seconds left!" Jonathan took a long shot, tossing the gift wrap into the recycling box. "The crowd is on their feet. They never . . . ooh!" Jonathan winced as a dark object hit the picture window with a thud. He peered through the glass and pointed to a tiny brown sparrow lying motionless in the snow. "Look! He hurt himself on the window. And . . . and now he's going to get eaten." The neighbor's striped gray cat appeared suddenly, slinking across the driveway. It hunched down, like a stain against the snow, with its hard green eyes fixed on the bird.

Elizabeth didn't know Jonathan was gone until she heard the back door slam. He raced to the front of the house, sloshing through the snow in Pop's black galoshes. She ran into the kitchen and met him at the door. Jonathan held the bird cupped in his hands. Its tiny chest fluttered up and down in faint whispers of breath.

"Do you think it's going to die?" asked Jonathan softly.

"Well, it's breathing, anyway. We'll keep it in the house to warm up. Hold on. We can use the basket Mom got for Christmas." Elizabeth set a roomy wicker basket on the kitchen table. She guided Jonathan's hands as he gently set the bird inside. "He needs to rest awhile," she said. "When he wakes up we can let him go. And as long as we're using Mom's Christmas presents, we can cover up the basket with this." She picked up a square pink scarf from the sofa and draped it over the basket.

Jonathan peeked under the scarf. "I'm naming him Mugsy."

"Uh . . . right. Well, we'd better leave Mugsy alone. We'll scare him if we get too close." She led Jonathan back into the living room.

Jonathan jumped up every few minutes to check on the bird. It still hadn't moved, but at least it was still breathing.

"My turn." Elizabeth tiptoed up to the table. She lifted the corner of the scarf, then squinted into the basket and groped around with her hand. "Jonathan! It's gone!"

"What?" Jonathan came running into the kitchen.

"The bird's gone. Look, the basket is empty."

"Pop's cat," moaned Jonathan. "We forgot about her. I bet she ate Mugsy." Their grandfather's portly black cat, officially known as Cat, was easy to forget. She had gone into hiding as soon as the first guests arrived on Christmas Eve. Jonathan slumped into a chair at the long kitchen table. "And now Mugsy's just a pile of feathers somewhere. And it's our fault."

Elizabeth's eyes searched the kitchen. "Don't worry. It wasn't the cat. The scarf wasn't even messed up. The bird must have gotten away by itself."

"But how could . . . Yahoo! Hit the dirt!" Jonathan dove to the floor, shouting and pointing his finger. "It's Mugsy! And he's coming in for a landing!" Mugsy shot into the kitchen like a dive bomber. After grazing the top of Elizabeth's ponytail, he clung to the kitchen curtain for a moment, then flew into the living room. He swept through the room, skimming the walls in a wide, frightened circle. Finally, he came to rest on the wooden frame of a large portrait hanging on the wall.

Elizabeth stood in the doorway. "Not a good idea, Mugsy. That's . . . that's Joshua Bailey!" The solemn, bearded man in the portrait was Pop's great grandfather. The painting was more than one hundred years old—Pop's prize possession. "Oh, no! Not that!" Elizabeth squeezed her eyes shut and counted to three. When she opened them again it was still there—an ugly white splat dribbling down the polished wood of the picture frame. "I'll tell you one thing, Jonathan. If we don't get this bird out of here, we are in big trouble.

I hope you won't mind spending the rest of your life in your room."

Elizabeth came up with a split-second plan. While Jonathan closed the curtains to keep the bird from hitting the window, she ran into the kitchen to get the pink scarf. She held it out in front of her, walking slowly, like a toreador approaching a bull.

"Don't worry, Mugsy. I'm just going to throw this over you and take you back outside." With the sparrow eyeing her nervously, she tossed the scarf up into the air. It floated down, empty, as the bird made an easy escape to the antlers hanging above the fireplace.

"Here. Let me do it. You gotta get wrist action." Jonathan grabbed the scarf and climbed up on a heavy chair next to the fireplace. "Three pointer!" He took aim and gave a mighty heave. The scarf ended up on the highest prong of the antlers. Mugsy flapped away and flew into a narrow den next to the living room. He headed for Pop's warrior mask collection, landing sideways on a hollow-eyed wooden face mounted on the wall.

"Hey, Elizabeth!" Jonathan, still perched on the chair, reached up behind a wooden pendulum clock on the mantel. "There's something up here." He pulled out a small white envelope propped up behind the clock. "The mystery letter!" He waved the paper in the air.

"Great. But forget it for now!" yelled Elizabeth. "Mugsy just flew in the den. And he . . . Not again!" Elizabeth groaned as she spotted a white splat on Pop's antique desk. "This is it, Jonathan! Bread and water for us!"

Elizabeth shot into the den and yanked the door shut. The wooden mask fell off the wall and crashed behind the couch. Mugsy fluttered away and sank his claws into a clump of hairy strings hanging from another mask. Elizabeth pressed her lips together and looked desperately around the room. The scarf idea would never work, but . . . the window. They were in luck. The den had an old crank window with no screen. Elizabeth used two hands to creak it open. A blast of cold air scattered the papers on Pop's desk.

"Okay, Mugsy. This is your chance." She clapped her hands

sharply and the bird took off again. This time it flew in a straight line out the window. "Jon, you can come in now." She lunged forward and cranked the window shut.

The two crowded up against the glass. Mugsy didn't stay around long. He flew up into a pine tree, pecked at his feathers indignantly, then flew away.

"Now, *that* was weird." Elizabeth sank into the soft cushions of Pop's old red couch. "The letter!" She bounced off as if she had sat on a thumb tack. "Where did you put the letter?"

"I left it up there." Standing in front of the fireplace, Jonathan stretched up and slipped the small envelope off the mantel. This was the mystery letter. No doubt about it. Their names were scrawled across the front. *Detectives Elizabeth and Jonathan Pollack.* The writing was odd, somehow—bold and yet shaky at the same time. As Jonathan tore open the envelope, Elizabeth looked up at the old pendulum clock. Usually she barely noticed its gentle sound, but now each tick sounded as sharp as the crack of a whip, as if the clock were hurrying them. Urging them on.

Jonathan pulled out a small sheet of plain white paper. As he unfolded the letter, Elizabeth read over his shoulder.

Dear Elizabeth and Jonathan,

Your grandfather told me of your interest in detective work and has sent me a newspaper article about the mystery you solved last summer. Congratulations on your good work! I understand you'll be staying at your grandfather's house for a few days after Christmas. I would be delighted if you could pay me a visit.

If you still like mysteries, I think you'll be interested to hear what I have to say.

All the best from
Poor Uncle Rudy
Rudolf Obermeyer

Elizabeth read the last sentence a second, then a third time. She had a tingly feeling, like being on a roller coaster just before it starts zooming downhill. She thought about last summer, when the old portrait on Pop's wall led them to a family secret and a long-forgotten mystery. Ever since then, Elizabeth had been waiting. She didn't know why or how, but she knew another mystery was going to find her.

Poor Uncle Rudy

"He didn't exactly say so, Jon, but I think we just got our second case." Elizabeth took the letter into her hand. "But I don't get it. We don't have an Uncle Rudy, and Mom and Dad don't either. So who is . . ." Elizabeth ran her finger under the large letters of the signature. "Who is *Poor Uncle Rudy Obermeyer*?"

"I know who he is!" Jonathan grabbed the fireplace tongs, clacking the bottoms together as he skipped around the coffee table. "He's really old, and he has white hair down to his knees. And he's a . . . prisoner in his own house, kept in a room in the basement." Jonathan began skipping faster and clacking louder. "And rats nibble his toes, and his beard is crawling with bugs. He's the only one who knows where the diamonds are hidden, but he'll never tell. So they keep him alive on water and . . . and chocolate-covered grasshoppers. And sometimes his beard gets to itching so bad he takes the bugs out and makes a —"

"Jonathan? What planet are you from? Anyway, put that thing down. I can't even think." Elizabeth grabbed the fireplace tongs. "Will you just try to be logical for a minute?" She dragged Jonathan into the kitchen and sat him down on a high-backed wooden chair. She did her best thinking at the long pine table. Gran used to complain that the kitchen was so old it should be in a museum. But Elizabeth liked the room just the way it was—soft and faded, like an old photograph. "Okay. Sit there and don't move. We're going to do this like Sherlock Holmes. We're going to look at the letter carefully and figure out some things." She set the letter on the table and sat down. "First of all, the envelope. What can you tell from the envelope?"

"I don't know. Looks like a rat might have nibbled the corner."

"Jon!"

"Okay. Okay. So . . . uh . . . I can tell where the letter is from, because of that thing stamped on the front. You know, the . . . "

"Postmark."

"Yeah." Jonathan leaned over. "It says *Milwaukee, WI.* That means Milwaukee, Wisconsin. And the writing on the address is kind of shaky, so I think Uncle Rudy is really old. Like Pop."

"Very good. You *might* be learning something." Elizabeth picked up the letter. *Rudolf Obermeyer.* I think that's a German name, so Uncle Rudy might be from Germany. Or at least his family came from there."

Elizabeth rubbed the paper between her thumb and forefinger. She wasn't sure why, but Sherlock Holmes always did things like that. "It's not fancy stationery or anything. Just a regular white piece of paper. And it's written in pencil, even the envelope. Maybe Uncle Rudy doesn't have much money, and that's why he signed himself *Poor Uncle Rudy.*"

Jonathan disappeared into the den and came back with a large map of Wisconsin. Elizabeth ran her finger across the southern border of the state until she found Lake Geneva. "Here's Williams Bay, where we are. Milwaukee's not too far away, so we could . . . Oh, no!" Elizabeth reached the window in one giant leap. "They're back! And we never cleaned up the bird mess." Pop's bulky blue Chevy, as wide as the street, chugged up the icy hill. Elizabeth could see her mother's short dark hair behind the steering wheel, and Pop next to her with a cigar in his mouth.

"Red Alert!" Elizabeth flew into action. She grabbed a fistful of rags from the back room and tossed one to Jonathan. "You wipe the desk and hang the mask back on the wall. I'll do the picture frame."

The back door opened just as the last white streak disappeared. Elizabeth heard Pop clatter into the kitchen, stomping the snow off his shoes and creaking across the wooden floor. She jabbed Jonathan with her elbow and pointed up to the pink scarf still dangling from the antlers.

"Where is everybody?" Pop's deep voice rolled out of the kitchen like a bowling ball.

"Uh . . . we're in here." Jonathan grabbed the fireplace tongs and stretched up to catch a tip of pink. He stuffed the scarf into the back of his pants while Elizabeth hid the rags underneath the fireplace logs. Pop walked into the room, puffing on the stub of a cigar. His wrinkled face peeked out between a plaid cap and a thick tweed coat that hung down to his shoes. Elizabeth tried not to think her grandfather looked like a hawk, but his nose—a strong nose, her mother called it—did look a little beakish.

"What were you doing in here?" Pop's pale blue eyes disappeared behind a suspicious squint. His glance wandered around the room and landed on Jonathan. "I thought I heard someone fooling with the fireplace tongs."

"Fireplace tongs?" Jonathan blinked innocently, as if he had never heard the word in his life.

"Don't worry, Pop. We weren't fooling around with anything," said Elizabeth. "And we have good news. We found the—"

"Come in the kitchen," interrupted Pop. "I want to show you something." Elizabeth shook her head as Pop shuffled out of the room. She knew he was hard of hearing, but it didn't make sense. He could hear the fireplace tongs clinking from the next room, but not what was said right in front of him.

As Mrs. Pollack came in with an armful of groceries, Pop slid something out of a paper bag. "I found your old detective sign taped up on the bedroom door," he said. "You're real detectives now, so you ought to have a real sign. I had it made specially." Pop held up a rectangular piece of honey-colored wood. Their names were grandly announced in graceful black letters. *Elizabeth and Jonathan Pollack. Ace Detectives for Hire.*

"It's great, Pop," said Elizabeth. "Just what we needed. Thanks."

"Yeah, cool!" Jonathan hopped over to take a closer look.

Elizabeth kept her eye on Pop. *Cool* was one of those words that could blast her grandfather into orbit. She waited for Lecture Number Ten: *there-are-more-than-500,000-words-in-the-English-language-and-all-you-can-say-is-cool.* But for once Pop seemed to forget about improving Jonathan's vocabulary.

"Well, I'm glad you like it."

"And we have a surprise, too," said Jonathan. "I think we have another case. We found that missing letter, and we have to visit someone."

Mrs. Pollack set down a bag of groceries with a sigh. Elizabeth noticed that her mother seemed to sigh a lot when they were at Pop's house. "I must be missing something here. You got a letter about a case?"

"It's from someone called Uncle Rudy," explained Elizabeth. "He heard about the mystery we solved, and he wants us to visit him. I think he wants to tell us something about another mystery. But we don't know who he is." She handed the letter to her mother while Pop went on a search for his glasses.

"Uncle Rudy? I can't believe it. I haven't seen him in years. He's not my real uncle, but he's an old friend of the family. His wife, too. Aunt Lorraine."

"Don't say any more, Mom," said Elizabeth. "We figured out some stuff and we—"

"*Deduced!*" called Pop from the next room. He walked into the kitchen with his reading glasses perched on his nose. "You didn't *figure out*. You *deduced* something from the letter. Never use a two-word verb, when one word will do. And forget *stuff*. It never adds anything."

Elizabeth had learned not to argue with Pop about words. Bad vocabulary was his pet peeve, along with mumbling, poor posture, and just about anything containing the word *video*. "Okay. Here's what we could *deduce*. We think he's old, because of his handwriting. And his name is German, so his family might have come from Germany. And we think he's probably poor."

Mrs. Pollack laughed. "Well, two out of three isn't bad. You're right about his age. Uncle Rudy's about the same age as Pop, so he'd be over eighty. And I think his grandparents were from Germany. But I wouldn't exactly call him poor. Actually, as far as I know, he's a millionaire."

Jonathan's eyebrows shot up. "A millionaire? You mean . . . a real millionaire?"

"That's right," said Mrs. Pollack. "Aunt Lorraine and Uncle Rudy own a chain of clothing stores in Milwaukee. He always signs his letters *Poor Uncle Rudy*. He's quite a joker." She turned to Pop. "Dad, do you remember the time he came to visit dressed up as a chauffeur and drove you to work in his Rolls Royce?"

Pop let out a low chuckle. "And Lorraine in the back seat with a maid's uniform on. Oh, we had some wild times when those two were around!"

Elizabeth looked at the letter. An eighty-year-old millionaire? Why would he want to talk to them?

"Milwaukee is about an hour away," said Mrs. Pollack. "I say we should go tomorrow morning."

Pop frowned. "Well, you can count me out. I've been having trouble with my knee again. You know I can't sit in a car that long." He turned away and faced the faded blue flowers on the wallpaper. "They hardly ever come to see me," he muttered. "Only two days left and they go traipsing off all over the state."

Elizabeth backed up and began studying the grocery bag. "We're going to help put things away, Jonathan. *Aren't* we." She thrust a can of green beans in his direction. It was better to leave delicate negotiations to their mother. Talking Pop into things was like steering an elephant through an obstacle course, and Mrs. Pollack was the only one who could do it. By the time the last bag was empty, the air had cleared. The three of them would go the next morning. Pop would stay home and rest his knee.

Pop waved his cigar as he walked out of the kitchen. "But you'd better get back by early afternoon. There's a lot of work to do, you know. Things need to be fixed up around here."

"Not *fixed up*," whispered Jonathan. "*Repaired.*"

Early the next morning Elizabeth awoke with the distinct feeling of being poked in the back by a spear. She gritted her teeth. Jonathan's doing, of course. She rolled over carefully and found herself eye to eye with a dark wooden mask from Pop's collection. It was the one that used to scare her, with a face stretched out thin and a hollow mouth that seemed about to moan. She plucked it up by the sharp chin and slid the mask under the bed.

Elizabeth considered immediate revenge—Pop's carved coconut that looked like a shrunken head would do nicely—but the icy darkness of the room kept her in bed. Besides, this would all go into the book she was planning. *Tales of the Weird*, she would call it. Starring Jonathan Pollack.

Elizabeth didn't even try to go back to sleep. She sank back into the softness of the old patchwork quilt. If only it were summer, she thought. She loved big, bright mornings, always ready and waiting as soon as she opened her eyes. Winter mornings were too pale and slow. And this day, of all days, had to get started. Elizabeth closed her eyes, making a mental check of the things in her backpack. Red spiral notebook. Lucky green pen. Magnifying glass. Uncle Rudy's letter. And of course her book, *How to Think Like a Detective*. She never went anywhere without that, even though she nearly had it memorized.

Nothing went fast at Pop's house, and it was well past eleven o'clock before they were finally on their way. Jonathan sat silently next to Elizabeth in the back seat. His hair had been severely wetted down and brushed, and he was consoling himself with his favorite book, *The Encyclopedia of the Totally Disgusting.*

Elizabeth tried to keep her mind on her detective handbook. She meant to read Chapter Three, *Interviewing a Client*, but the day was simply too beautiful to ignore. A fairy dust sparkle of new snow softened the hills, and the bold blue sky practically shouted for attention. The perfect day for starting a new mystery. Elizabeth Pollack, ace detective, and her trusty . . .

"Hey, Elizabeth, wanna see what lives in your pillow?" Jonathan, fully recovered from his mope, gurgled with delight over a full-page picture in his book. "Dust mites. They're all over the place. Gazillions of 'em. They're really small, but the picture shows them close up. So you get to see what they look like." Out of the corner of her eye Elizabeth could see the thing—an eight-legged beast with a hairless, bloated body and a pinpoint of a head. Jonathan tried to stick the book under her nose, but Elizabeth pushed it away like a piece of rotten meat. *The Encyclopedia of the Totally Disgusting* was her curse. A thousand times she had hidden that book. A thousand times Jonathan had found it.

"They like to eat dead skin. And I bet they live in your hair, too." Jonathan squinted and pretended to pick something out of her ponytail.

Elizabeth took three deep breaths and managed to talk Jonathan into listening to a book on tape. By the time they reached Milwaukee, he had not mentioned the word *dust mite* for forty-five minutes.

"Hurry up and look out the window, kids," said Mrs. Pollack for the second time. "You can see the skyline of Milwaukee."

Elizabeth caught a glimpse of a thick tower with clocks on all four sides. Here and there, church spires rose up among serious-looking brick factories. After slowing down in the tangle of city streets, Mrs. Pollack pulled into an underground parking garage. A thin, blond-haired man in a brown uniform whipped open the car doors with a flourish. "Lakeview Towers," he announced. He pointed the way to the elevator before parking the car for them.

"Hey, pretty fancy. Twenty-five floors." Jonathan stared at the long row of buttons in the elevator. In their Indiana hometown, the tallest building was only four stories high.

The elevator whisked them up to the top floor with no stops. As they made their way down a narrow carpeted hallway, Mrs. Pollack dug a square of paper from her coat pocket. "2507. This is it." She gave the shiny brass door knocker two quick taps, and almost at once the door swung open. Elizabeth half expected a crusty old butler with white gloves, but the door was opened by a small, smartly-dressed woman. Her hair was swept up into a crown of carefully arranged gray curls.

"The Pollack Detective Agency, if I'm not mistaken." She spoke with the hint of a smile as she gave each of them a brisk handshake. "I'm Mrs. Dornan, the Obermeyers' housekeeper. Come right on in. Mr. Obermeyer is expecting you."

She led them around the corner into a large, sunny living room. Elizabeth stopped in the doorway, blinking into the brightness like a mole popped up in the sunlight. She had never seen such a room, except maybe in fancy magazines people keep on their coffee tables. Everything was a soft, creamy white—the curtains, the carpet, even the sofa and chairs. All that was missing was an angel playing the harp.

Jonathan, for once in his life, stood perfectly still. He stared out the window—a wall of windows, really. Outside was a riot of bright blue sky. In the distance, Lake Michigan stretched out as big as the sea.

Mrs. Pollack was already greeting Uncle Rudy, who had risen from the couch. Elizabeth could hardly believe he was eighty. For one thing, he looked as tall as a tree, and his hair was jet black, a kind of wet-looking black that probably came from a bottle. His face didn't have wrinkles like Pop's, just two deep canyons angling down from his cheeks.

"Glad you could come. Glad you could come." Uncle Rudy directed Elizabeth and Jonathan into two snow white arm chairs.

"I'm sorry my wife couldn't be here. She has a doctor's appointment."

Mrs. Pollack and Uncle Rudy soon fell into a lively conversation, talking and laughing about old times. Elizabeth didn't follow the story, but it had something to do with Pop wearing a hula skirt. She gave up trying to picture that. Finally, with no end in sight, she rustled her backpack, hoping her mother would get the hint.

It worked. After one hearty laugh, Uncle Rudy trumpeted a few times into a large handkerchief, then turned to Elizabeth and Jonathan. "Well, I suppose you're wondering why an old man you don't even know has asked you to come and see him."

He leaned forward in his chair, fixing them with his keen brown eyes. "Let me get right to the point. It has to do with a set of coins. Five gold coins—over a thousand years old. They were passed down in my family for generations. But after my father died, they were never found. They've been missing now for many years."

Suddenly, Uncle Rudy straightened up and pulled a checkbook out of his pocket. "I'd like to hire you two to find those coins," he said matter-of-factly. He looked up, his pen poised for writing. "Name your fee," he commanded. "Just name your fee."

Uncle Rudy's Tale

"Our . . . fee?" Elizabeth tried to sound professional, but the words slipped out in a nervous squeak. With a stab of alarm, she thought about their detective sign at Pop's house. *Elizabeth and Jonathan Pollack. Ace Detectives for Hire.* What if Uncle Rudy knew about the sign? Maybe he thought they were looking for a job.

"Well, I . . ." Elizabeth looked around for help. Mrs. Pollack sat silently, fighting back a smile with a slight twitch of her lips. As for Jonathan, he had suddenly decided his shoelaces needed to be undone and retied.

"You see," said Elizabeth, "we're really just . . . I mean, we did solve that one mystery about the portrait. But we've never had a real job or anything."

"Yeah, maybe you should hire some real, grown-up detectives," said Jonathan. He glanced up from his shoelaces.

"Real detectives?" Uncle Rudy gave a snort and slapped the air with his large hands. "I hired real detectives years ago. Didn't find out a thing. I need someone with fresh ideas. Someone whose mind isn't all cluttered up with other things."

Mrs. Pollack finally spoke up. "Uncle Rudy, I think it's the part about being hired for money that's bothering them. They would feel under pressure."

"No problem. No problem at all. We'll forget about a fee. Tell you what. If you find those coins, there'll be a $500 reward for each of you. And if you don't, we'll chalk it up to experience." Uncle Rudy put the checkbook into his pocket. "Now, you'll need to come back to Milwaukee to do your investigation. I'll pay your expenses, of course. You can stay at The Edwardian. Best hotel in town. How does that sound?"

Elizabeth clutched the arms of the chair. She needed to anchor herself. Otherwise she might just float up to the ceiling like a helium balloon. Missing coins. Five hundred dollar reward. Best hotel in town. It was a first class, tiptop mystery. But she wasn't so sure about the Pollack Detective Agency. She was only eleven, and Jonathan was about as helpful as an untrained puppy. She would have to shape him up fast. "It sounds good," she said hesitantly. "But I think we need to know more."

"No problem," said Uncle Rudy. "No problem at all. Let me start from the beginning, then you can decide."

Before he could continue, Mrs. Dornan appeared in the doorway with a large silver tray.

"Crab legs," whispered Jonathan. "That's what rich people eat. And piles and piles of little black fish eggs."

"Sorry, no caviar today," laughed Mrs. Dornan. "We thought you might like these better." She set the tray down on a long, low coffee table. On it was a pitcher of milk and a mountain of peanut butter and jelly sandwiches.

Uncle Rudy balanced a plate on his knees and quickly polished off two sandwiches. Elizabeth gulped down one sandwich, then opened her red detective notebook. As she clicked her pen, six words flowed out as if they were writing themselves on the page. *The Mystery of the Ancient Coins.* Strange. The words had a kind of power. Elizabeth knew the Pollack Detective Agency had taken the case.

Uncle Rudy set down his empty glass on the tray. "Well, I guess I might as well start at the very beginning. You see, my family, the Obermeyers, originally came from Bavaria. That's the southern part of Germany. About two hundred years ago, one of my ancestors found five gold coins in a field he was plowing. They were very old, probably Roman. Ever since then the coins have been passed down in the family from generation to generation. When my grandfather came to America, he brought the coins with him. They were passed down to my father, and they were supposed to be passed down to me."

"What happened?" asked Jonathan.

Uncle Rudy paused. "To tell you the truth, I never took much interest in the coins. Too busy with my own life. My father used to show them to me, and I know he meant for me to have them. But after he died, I couldn't find the coins anywhere. They've never been found."

"Wait. Time out." Elizabeth held up her left hand while she continued to write. "Let me catch up." Her detective handbook said the first interview is the most important. But Uncle Rudy's words were racing by, and she could only plod along in her tortoise-slow cursive. "Okay. I'm caught up." She put down her pen and shook out her hand. "But didn't your father tell you where he kept the coins?"

"Not exactly. After my mother died, my father took an apartment in a retirement home in downtown Milwaukee. The King's Home for Retired Gentlemen. Not long after he moved there, we spoke on the telephone and he talked about the coins. He said . . ." Uncle Rudy closed his eyes and rubbed his forehead. "I'm trying to remember the words he used. *The coins are in a safe place,* he said. *I'll have to show you the hidden key.* Yes, that was it. *I'll have to show you the hidden key.* I'm afraid that's the only clue."

Elizabeth wrote the words of the clue with a double underline. Jonathan was quiet, but he had inched forward in his armchair and sat crouched on the very edge.

"But what does the key open?" asked Mrs. Pollack.

"That's just it," said Uncle Rudy. "I never followed up on it. Never asked him about it. Time went by and then he was gone. It was too late." Uncle Rudy's voice was flat. "Too late for a lot of things. I never found the key. I never found the coins. They were passed down for over 150 years, and I broke the chain."

Uncle Rudy was silent for a moment, then brightened up. "But it may not be too late to find the coins. You see, the King's Home still exists. Maybe you could search there again. And then there's my daughter Zina. She has all my father's furniture, some beautiful old pieces. I'm sure she wouldn't mind if you looked at them. Maybe I didn't search thoroughly enough."

"Did you check for secret compartments?" asked Jonathan. "Pop says most old furniture has secret places where people used to hide things."

"There you go!" Uncle Rudy slapped his knee. "Now that's a fresh idea. Didn't even occur to me, or to those bonehead detectives I hired. All they could tell me was they didn't think the coins had been stolen."

Uncle Rudy sat back and stretched out his long legs. "Let me tell you why I wrote to you. A few weeks ago, I happened to be at the King's Home visiting a friend. And I thought to myself, if I had a young pair of eyes and a young pair of legs, I'd have another go at finding those coins. Then I came home, and what did I find? A Christmas card from your grandfather telling me all about the family mystery you solved last summer." Uncle Rudy lowered his voice. "Then all of a sudden one of my flashes came over me. You see, sometimes I get these feelings, like a flashbulb going off in my head. They tell me just the right thing to do. And my feelings told me you were the ones who could help me. I never ignore my flashes."

Jonathan's limbs began to wiggle. Elizabeth could nearly see the flashbulbs going off in *his* head. He half tumbled out of the chair. "We'll take the case! And we'll find the coins!"

By the time they had asked a few more questions, Elizabeth had filled two pages of her notebook. Uncle Rudy's father, Wilhelm Obermeyer, was a tailor who eventually opened up his own small department store in Milwaukee. After his wife died, he had lived at King's Home for the last two years of his life. Jonathan asked if Rudy's father had any hobbies (Elizabeth had rolled her eyes at this question), and Uncle Rudy told them that his father liked reading and word puzzles.

"Wait a minute," said Elizabeth. "We don't even know what the coins look like. My detective handbook says you should always know exactly what you're looking for."

"You're right." Uncle Rudy shook his head in delight. "I can tell you're a sharp one. Now if I remember right the coins are small, about the size of a dime, but made of gold. Let's see. Some of them just had a fancy design on them, and one or two had a bird's head. And there was something different about the coins. You see, they weren't flat. They were all shaped like . . . like little saucers. My father called them rainbow cup coins."

"Rainbow cup coins," repeated Mrs. Pollack. "What a beautiful name."

Uncle Rudy lifted himself off the couch and motioned for them to follow. In the front hallway across from the door, he knelt down in front of a long dark chest. He lifted the heavy cover and leaned inside. "I keep some of my grandmother's things in here," he said. "And there's something that may help you. A drawing of one of the coins. Ah, here it is." Underneath a dark-colored patchwork quilt and a tiny pair of satin wedding shoes was a small book bound in splotchy brown leather.

"This is my Grandmother Johanna's journal," he said as he slowly stood up. "She drew a little picture of a rainbow cup coin. Yes, right here." He held the book open to a page with a small pencil drawing at the top. "The writing is in German though. Can't read a word of it myself."

"Then you've come to the right detectives," said Mrs. Pollack. "We lived in Germany for a whole year. That was two years ago when I was doing some research for a book. The kids went to school there." She turned to Elizabeth and Jonathan. "They've kept up with their German pretty well. I think they can still read it."

"So . . . they read German." Uncle Rudy's face tightened into a frown. It lasted only an instant, like a cloud scurrying across the sun on a windy day. But Elizabeth had noticed. She gazed at the neat black letters on the open page of the diary. Was there something Uncle Rudy didn't want them to read?

"Well, there you go!" Uncle Rudy was at full sail once again. "I knew you were sharp ones. My flashes are always right, I tell you." He handed the diary to Elizabeth. "Maybe you can make some sense out of this. You just keep it as long as you need to."

He helped them on with their coats. "I'd just like to get those coins back, that's all."

"I'm afraid your detectives won't be able to come back to Milwaukee until spring vacation," said Mrs. Pollack. "How about if we come back in March?"

"Just send me the dates," said Uncle Rudy. "I'll fix you up with a deluxe suite. Room service and all the trimmings."

As they waited for the elevator doors to open, Uncle Rudy's voice boomed into the hallway. "No problem. No problem at all!"

"I want to compliment you on your behavior, Jonathan," said Mrs. Pollack. "You were very polite and a good listener."

Just wait, thought Elizabeth. Her brother had sat still for over an hour. She knew the strain would be too much. Sure enough, Jonathan's face began changing, like a werewolf under a full moon. He bugged his eyes out and pumped Elizabeth's arm up and down. "Muh-nee. Muh-nee. Muh-nee." He spoke with a dopey, half hysterical laugh. "I buy whoopee cushions. I buy fake teeth. I buy rubber vomit."

Elizabeth pulled away and fled into the elevator. "Jonathan, you are sick."

She stood next to her mother with her back toward Jonathan as the elevator purred down twenty-five floors. In a matter of seconds the doors slid open onto the dimly lit parking garage. Elizabeth shuffled out and stood still for a moment. She took two deep breaths, waiting for her stomach to come back down from the top floor.

Jonathan and Mrs. Pollack walked on, looking for the parking attendant. Elizabeth didn't follow them. She had already spotted their small red car at the end of the aisle. But who was . . . ? She pushed up her glasses and leaned forward. Someone was standing behind their car—a short man in a blue parka. He seemed to be writing on a small pad of paper in his hand. He must have heard the elevator doors close, for suddenly he turned toward Elizabeth. His startled and angry look made her take a step back. Without a word, he stuffed the paper into his pocket and disappeared through a door marked *Stairway.*

Elizabeth stared as the gray metal door clicked shut. She knew what the man had been doing. For some reason—she couldn't begin to imagine why—the strange man in the blue parka had been copying down their license number.

The Old Clock Man

The bang of the metal door was followed by quick footsteps, then the sound of another door slamming shut. Elizabeth held her breath and strained her ears, but she could hear only the kettledrum pounding of her own heart. When she was sure the man was gone, she pulled her notebook from her backpack. She knew what she had to do. *Top Ten Tips for Detectives.* They were written in bold print in her detective handbook. She had read them a thousand times. *Number five. Human memory is frail and fades quickly. Making a written record immediately after the event can save details that would otherwise be lost.*

Elizabeth had to squeeze her pen hard to keep from trembling. She printed in small, tight letters: *short man, dark blue parka, small nose, small eyes, dark hair, no hat. In his fifties, maybe older. Had a small notebook in his hand.* Elizabeth leaned against the wall. Things were happening almost too fast. First a millionaire offers them a reward to find five missing coins, and now a mysterious man writes down their license number.

"Hey, asparagus-legs, how come you're glued to the wall?" Elizabeth turned to see Jonathan walking toward the car with their mother. No one in the world could bring her to a boil faster than her brother, but for once, she was grateful. It was better to be mad than scared. She gave him the big-sister look—eyes narrowed, lip slightly curled.

"It just so happens that I saw something very mysterious." She turned to her mother. "There was a man. He was standing behind our car copying down our license number. And when he saw me he ran away."

Mrs. Pollack muttered a vague "Oh, really." She patted Elizabeth's arm. "Probably just someone who works for the apartment building."

"But, Mom. Why would someone . . ." No use finishing. Elizabeth could see that her mother and Jonathan were in the middle of a discussion. Jonathan was begging for something, and when Jonathan got in the begging mood, he turned into the all-time champion whiner of the United States of America, probably of the whole world. This time he was pleading with Mrs. Pollack to go straight to Rudy's daughter's house. "Please, Mom. Please. I could find those coins right now. I know they're in that old furniture she has. And then we could get the reward right away."

Mrs. Pollack opened up the car and climbed in. "I already told you, Jonathan. We have to get back. You know how upset Pop gets when we're late." She pulled the car out of the parking garage and ordered Jonathan not to say another word. Otherwise she would have to take away his favorite book.

Elizabeth spent a moment pleasantly imagining *The Encyclopedia of the Totally Disgusting* being locked forever in a vault. The walls, she decided, would be two-feet thick and made of steel. Dynamite-proof, of course. With a contented sigh, she brought her mind back to the case of the missing coins. Maybe she could get in a little detective training before Jonathan began enlightening her about dust mites.

"Anyway, Jon, it's not a good idea to look for the coins right away. My detective handbook says you're not supposed to do anything until you gather all kinds of information. Here. Listen to this." At the sight of Elizabeth's book, Jonathan held his ears, and began to hum loudly. Elizabeth turned toward him and trumpeted her message across the back seat. *"Background information is an important, but often neglected, part of an investigation. A good investigator casts a wide net, gathering as much information as possible before taking action. Details which at first seem unimportant may later prove to be the key that unlocks the mystery.* So that means . . ."* She gave his shoulder a vigorous shake. "We shouldn't be looking all over for the coins until we've gotten more information and thought things over. We need to read this old diary, for one thing. And talk to someone who knows about old coins. And we may have some more questions for Uncle Rudy."

Elizabeth decided to give up on Jonathan's training. For now at least. She took the old diary out of her backpack and opened it to the page Uncle Rudy had marked. She stared at the page for a moment, then turned to another page and another. "Mom, are you sure this is written in German? It's really weird. I can't read this writing. Not one word."

"Oh, wait a minute. I know what the problem is," said Mrs. Pollack. "That diary is from the 1800s. It must be written in the old German script. It's a kind of handwriting that isn't used in Germany anymore. Completely different from what you learned."

"Oh, great!" said Elizabeth. "So how are we going to read this?"

"The only thing I can think of is to find an older person who comes from Germany. Someone who might have learned the old handwriting as a child. I don't know. Maybe Pop can help you."

Less than an hour later, they pulled into Pop's steep driveway. Jonathan hopped out of the car but didn't get any farther than the kitchen window. "Stormy waters ahead!" He gave his report as he ran back to the car. "Pop's sitting at the kitchen table and he's wearing his hat and coat. And he doesn't look too happy."

Jonathan and Elizabeth stayed behind their mother as she went in the back door. "What in blazes took you so long?" sputtered Pop. "I need to get a haircut and I want to go now."

Mrs. Pollack sat at the kitchen table. She soon convinced Pop to take off his hat and coat and let her take a rest. "Anyway, the kids have some news for you."

Pop sat stiffly at first, but by the time Mrs. Pollack was finished resting, he was huddled over the diary, slowly turning the pages.

"We told Pop all about the mystery," said Jonathan. "And we have a plan. Pop needs a haircut, but we can't go to the barber in Williams Bay. He's mad at Pop for being so crabby, and he says he won't cut his hair anymore."

Mrs. Pollack looked at Pop and shook her head. "Don't tell me any more until I sit down."

"So you have to drive us to a barbershop in Walworth," continued Jonathan. "That way Elizabeth and I can go see Mr. Lattimore, because his shop is right around the corner."

"We're going to interview him about how to find secret hiding places in old furniture," said Elizabeth.

Mrs. Pollack nodded. Mr. Lattimore was a special friend who repaired antique furniture. In his cluttered shop, Elizabeth and Jonathan had started on their first mystery.

"And then we have to go see someone else," added Elizabeth. "Pop knows a man who fixes clocks. He comes from Germany, and Pop thinks he's about seventy-five years old. He probably learned the old handwriting when he was in school. So he could read that page in the diary."

Mrs. Pollack looked at her watch. "I don't know. Seems like an awfully full agenda for so late in the afternoon."

Elizabeth signaled Jonathan with a slight twitch of her eyebrows. Time to use the secret charm their mother could never resist. "We ordered four bratwurst dinners at the fire station," said Jonathan. "Some kind of fund-raiser. So you don't have to make dinner."

"Well now, that sounds better," said Mrs. Pollack. "Suddenly I'm getting into the detective mood."

On the town square in Walworth, Mrs. Pollack parked the car in front of a tiny barber shop.

"We'll meet you back here," called Elizabeth. "As soon as we're done." She and Jonathan hurried away, following the narrow sidewalk around the corner to Mr. Lattimore's shop. The front room with the long wooden counter was empty, as usual, but they could see someone working in the back room. There was no mistaking Mr. Lattimore. He was a bulky man with a fierce pair of dark eyebrows. He looked up from the chair he was sanding and motioned them in with a wave of his meaty hand.

"Well, if it isn't the two famous detectives!" He put both hands to his forehead and closed his eyes. "Don't tell me. I see it all. You're working on another case and you're here to interview me again."

"How did you know?" laughed Elizabeth. She stepped over a dresser drawer as she made her way into the workshop.

"Just a little deduction of my own. I saw you were carrying your detective notebook."

"We do want to interview you," said Jonathan. "And we have another case. We're looking for some gold coins that got lost a long time ago, and we're going to get a reward."

"*If* we find them, that is," added Elizabeth.

Mr. Lattimore pulled up three rickety wooden chairs. "You're not kidding, are you?"

"No, we're not," said Elizabeth. She opened up her notebook. "We think the coins might be hidden in some old furniture, or at least there might be a key hidden there. So we need to know how to find secret hiding places."

Jonathan and Elizabeth soon discovered they had come to the right person. Mr. Lattimore had worked with antiques for years, and he had found secret compartments containing everything from money and old letters to a rock-hard piece of Swiss cheese. Within fifteen minutes, he had given them a quick course on exploring old furniture.

"Always start by taking the drawers out," he said, "and look over every inch of the shell with a flashlight. Never assume anything is solid. A wooden panel can be the front of a hidden drawer. And don't forget to measure how deep the drawers are. If they look the same on the outside but one is more shallow, it may have a false bottom." Elizabeth was still scribbling in her notebook when Jonathan mumbled a hurried thanks and dashed out the door.

"Hey, wait up," she yelled.

"I'm going to the barber shop," he called over his shoulder. "I think they have candy there."

Elizabeth said good-bye to Mr. Lattimore and walked out into the twilight. Vaguely, she noticed a man standing on the sidewalk farther down the street. As she closed the door behind her, he turned around quickly and walked into a shop. Elizabeth didn't know why she felt a sudden sting of fear. The man's hurried movements, perhaps. Or the cold loneliness of the empty street.

Elizabeth stepped back closer to Mr. Lattimore's shop. She wanted to follow Jonathan, but she couldn't. Not yet. There was one thing she had to find out about that man. She stiffened the back of her knees and forced herself forward. The man had entered a small toy store just up the street. She edged her way toward the shop, keeping close to the buildings. Elizabeth felt like a real detective now. She also felt completely idiotic, creeping around the town square as if she were stalking the FBI's most wanted.

She crouched down and peered in past a large doll house in the display window. The man was standing at the counter with his back toward her. One glimpse told her what she needed to know. He was short and he was wearing a parka. Dark blue.

Elizabeth turned and hurried down the street at a slow run, taking in icy sharp breaths of air. Once in sight of the barber shop, she slowed down to a walk. What was wrong with her anyway? The man had done nothing more than turn around quickly and walk into a store, she told herself. And hundreds, maybe even thousands, of men wore dark blue parkas on a cold winter night in Wisconsin.

All the same, Elizabeth was glad to step into the bright warmth of the barber shop. She took a deep breath, letting the cold edge of fear soften and fade. She felt safe here. The place was as snug as a pocket, a clutter of bottles and jars and sweet-smelling things. Pop had been neatly trimmed and dusted with powder, and was being helped out of the chair by Mrs. Pollack. Jonathan, with a lollipop in his mouth, was slouched behind a comic book.

"Sounds like your interview went well," said Mrs. Pollack.

"Oh . . . yeah. Fine." Elizabeth picked up a magazine and decided not to think about blue parkas. "Can we go see that German man now?"

A few minutes later, Pop directed Mrs. Pollack onto a small road just outside of town. The hills were gone now, faded away into the deep winter night. A faint sprinkling of stars shimmered across the sky.

"Now when we get there," said Pop, "someone else had better do the talking. Mrs. Kruger is a little put out with me."

Elizabeth couldn't see her mother's face, but she knew she was rolling her eyes. "So what did you do to make Mrs. Kruger mad?" asked Mrs. Pollack.

"I gave her some advice, that's all. A little friendly advice. I told her she'd look a heck of a lot better if she put on some make-up. And quit wearing those dumpy dresses with no waist." Elizabeth couldn't see Pop's face either, but she knew he was sitting up straight and jutting his chin out. He always did that when he was defending himself.

"Oh, Dad," groaned Mrs. Pollack, "why do you have to say things like that?"

"Because it's the truth. People need to hear the truth. So they can improve themselves."

"Well, do me a favor," said Mrs. Pollack. "Just don't tell the truth when we get there. I mean . . . oh, you know what I mean."

Elizabeth caught herself sighing just like her mother. Why did Pop always have to be improving people? Why couldn't he just do regular things like regular grandfathers? Fishing or woodworking, maybe. Or building a mini Eiffel Tower out of match sticks. At least that would keep him out of trouble.

Mrs. Pollack pulled down a driveway leading to a tidy white clapboard house. A small circle of light lit up a sign in the front yard. *The Old Clock Man.* The four of them climbed out of the warm car and plunged again into the frigid night.

Pop opened the door to a small shop attached to the house. They were greeted by a blast of hot air and the sweet, oily smell of a kerosene heater. Along the walls were clocks of every shape and size, each ticking at its own pace and filling the room with a nervous flutter of sound.

A woman sitting behind the counter looked up from her account book. She was in her late sixties, a solid, heavyset woman. Her face reddened when she set eyes on Pop.

Without a word, she got up and stood in the doorway which led into the house. "Gustav," she called. "Someone to see you." With that, she stomped out of the room.

Pop turned to the others and moved his lips in a loud whisper. "Mrs. Kruger. Still mad."

A few moments later Mr. Kruger stepped into the room. His pleasant face clouded over immediately. "So. Mr. Emerson. Are we going to behave today or do we argue?" He spoke quickly, but with a thick German accent.

Pop raised his right hand and stared straight ahead. "I'm going to be on my best behavior," he said solemnly. "I've sworn not to tell the truth."

Mrs. Pollack gave a hint of a smile, but Mr. Kruger didn't seem to think Pop was funny. "So you have a clock for me to fix?" he asked gruffly.

Mrs. Pollack stepped forward. "*Guten Abend, Herr Kruger.*" Mr. Kruger's eyes sparkled with delight—Mrs. Pollack had wished him a good evening in German. After a short conversation in his native language, he couldn't stop smiling. "Anna," he called. "The lady speaks German."

Elizabeth put the diary on the counter and opened it to the page with the drawing of a coin. "Actually, we wanted to ask you a favor," she said hesitantly. "You see, my brother and I are . . . well, we do detective work. We're helping a friend find some old German coins that were lost years and years ago. We're trying to find out all we can about the coins, and we know there's something written about them in this diary. But it was written a long time ago, and we can't read a word. It's written in an old kind of writing they don't teach anymore."

Mr. Kruger put on a pair of half glasses and picked up the diary.

"*Ach, die alte deutsche Schrift,* the old German writing." He turned to Elizabeth. "This is the kind of handwriting I learned as a child."

"Could you read us the part that talks about the coins?" asked Jonathan.

"And translate it, too, please," added Elizabeth. "Our German's a little rusty."

Mr. Kruger sat down and took a few minutes to read the page. "Yes, quite interesting," he said. "This page is dated January 2, 1885, and it tells the story of the coins you're looking for. It says there were five gold coins found in 1789 by a farmer named August Obermeyer. That was in Graberstadt in Bavaria. *Ja,* and the coins are very old, maybe even Roman. Let's see. They were passed down in the family and brought to America by Franz Obermeyer in 1850." Mr. Kruger turned the page.

"Does it say anything else?" asked Elizabeth. She wrote down the names in her notebook, but it was just a more detailed version of what Uncle Rudy had already told them.

"Well, let me look. It says there are many legends and superstitions about the coins." Mr. Kruger read on to himself, then looked up uncertainly.

"Is that all?" asked Jonathan.

Mr. Kruger shrugged his shoulders. "Oh, the rest is just *Märchen*—old fairy tales. Nothing worth knowing."

"No, tell us," said Elizabeth. "Please. We want to know everything we can about the coins, even if it's just a story."

"Well," said Mr. Kruger, "the rainbow cup coins are said to bring

luck and good fortune to the family, but they must be treasured and cared for well. If not, the family will come under . . . how do you say it, under a kind of curse."

Mr. Kruger paused. His audience was spellbound. Even Mrs. Kruger had returned and stood in the doorway.

"According to the legend," he continued, "if the coins are lost, they *must* be found before forty years have passed. If not, a great misfortune will befall the family. But once the coins are lost, finding them will be difficult, very difficult. It is said they can only be found . . ." He paused, then spoke slowly. "They can only be found by a person with a heart that dares to face . . . danger."

Mr. Kruger's last word fell like a stone. Elizabeth stood perfectly still. The ticking of the old clocks on the wall grew louder and louder, until the sound seemed to be pounding inside her. Or was it the quickening beat of her own heart?

Disturbing Information

"Bunk and balderdash! That's what I say. Those old superstitions are just bunk and balderdash. And that curse. Don't you believe a word of it!" Pop was sitting at his kitchen table, polishing off the remains of a bratwurst dinner. He finished his meal with a flourish, dropping his knife and fork noisily onto the plate.

"Oh, who cares about the curse anyway?" said Jonathan. He took aim and speared the last crispy potato pancake. "We're going to find the coins. So what does it matter? A heart that dares to face danger. That's me, all right."

Elizabeth was only half listening. She was beginning to think she liked pretend cases better, cases without curses and warnings of danger, or men in blue parkas hanging about.

"I don't know," she said. "I don't believe in curses, but it still gives me a creepy feeling. What if we don't find the coins?"

"All I can say is, don't dwell on it," said Pop. "Just don't dwell on it." He sat back in his chair and gave a kingly wave of his hand. That meant his plate should now be cleared from the table. "And get me my cigars," he called to Jonathan, who was carrying the plate to the sink. Jonathan shuffled over to Pop with his eyes cast down to the ground. "Your humble servant," he said as he held out the box of cigars.

Jonathan looked at Elizabeth and tapped the tip of his nose with his index finger. It was their sign for *Pop's-going-to-fill-the room-with-smoke-so-we'd-better-get-out-of-here.* "Uh, Jonathan and I need to work on the case," said Elizabeth quickly. "And you said we could call Dad and tell him about what happened today." She and Jonathan ducked underneath a billowing cloud of cigar smoke and hurried out of the kitchen.

It wasn't long before Elizabeth was calling her mother to come up and say goodnight.

"I'm not used to this," said Mrs. Pollack as she walked into the bedroom. "Jonathan went to sleep on his own, and you're volunteering to go to bed."

"Yeah, I guess it was a long day," said Elizabeth. After her mother left, Elizabeth curled up under the patchwork quilt. Gentle nighttime sounds drifted up the stairs. Pop's footsteps padded across the living room, the lock on the front door clicked, Cat ventured out of her hiding place and meowed for attention. Elizabeth could hear Pop's voice, softer and not so bossy, as he talked and laughed with Mrs. Pollack.

The sleepy ticking of the mantel clock brought Elizabeth back to the old clock shop. What would happen when people like Mr. Kruger weren't around anymore? Who would be able to read the old German writing? Memory keepers. Just like her mother said. Some people have to hold onto knowledge, keep the old ways alive so they don't get lost. Maybe somewhere there were memory keepers still teaching the old writing. She hoped so, anyway.

The old writing . . . Elizabeth closed her eyes, feeling herself slip deeper and deeper into the dark warmth of the bed. Why worry about the curse anyway? Uncle Rudy's father died so long ago, the forty years must have already passed by, and nothing bad had happened. Elizabeth would have fallen asleep with that comforting thought if the *Top Ten Tips for Detectives* hadn't made her eyes pop open. *How to Think Like a Detective. Tip Number Nine. Detectives do not make assumptions; detectives check facts.*

Exactly how long ago did Uncle Rudy's father die? Elizabeth

squeezed her eyes shut and turned over twice, but ignoring the question was like trying to walk with a stone in her shoe. She had to know right now.

She leaned over and dug her flashlight and detective notebook out of her backpack. She had written down the date of his death. All she had to do was subtract. She did the math four times, but it always came out the same. Uncle Rudy's father had died thirty-nine years ago. In three months it would be forty years. Elizabeth gazed at the cold gleam of moonlight on the patchwork quilt. Did Uncle Rudy know about the curse? Is that why he was suddenly so interested in finding the coins?

The next morning Elizabeth was glad for the big helping of new snow that fell during the night. When she sailed down the hill on Pop's old wooden sled, she was worry-free. No mystery. No puzzles. No curses. For a time, at least.

On the morning they were to leave, Pop was extra cranky, grumbling from room to room like an unhappy bumble bee. He was always like that when they were getting ready to leave. Mrs. Pollack said it was his way of showing he didn't want them to go.

"You can't leave yet. I need someone to go into the closet and get something." Jonathan was happy to volunteer. He followed Pop into the back room off the kitchen and crawled into a long, narrow closet.

"Farther back!" called Pop. "There's a box underneath the coats." With his knees full of dust, Jonathan came out dragging a box that had never been opened.

Pop removed a cassette tape recorder from the box and set it on the kitchen table, poking and squinting as if he were examining an alien spaceship. "How do you work this blasted thing, anyway?" Pop didn't say much, but he had some mysterious project in mind. He also wanted to know if he could keep the old diary for awhile. Elizabeth gladly gave it up. The diary had already told her more than she wanted to know.

When it was time to leave, Pop wrapped himself in his long

tweed coat and gave each of them a stiff hug before they climbed into the car. As Mrs. Pollack backed down the long, steep driveway, he shouted out his standard list of warnings and driving tips. "Keep to the left! To the left, I said! Watch that garbage can!" Pop waved both arms in the air. "And don't run out of gas." When Elizabeth turned around for the last time, Pop wasn't waving anymore. He stood at the top of the driveway, his arms at his sides, staring alone into the winter morning.

By the time they reached central Indiana, the snow had all but disappeared. Only a few lonely white patches littered the jagged fields of corn stubble.

Mr. Pollack stepped out the back door just as they pulled into the driveway of their brick house. He was a tall, willowy man, with light brown hair just like Jonathan's, except slightly better behaved. Elizabeth was surprised to see him wearing his white lab coat.

"Welcome home! I've been experimenting with something in the kitchen."

"Oh." Mrs. Pollack gave a brave smile. "Something from the science conference?"

Jonathan leaped out of the car and hurried into the kitchen. Last year Mr. Pollack had come back from the teachers' meeting with an ant farm and a tub of garbage-eating worms. Elizabeth peeked into the kitchen and saw Jonathan sitting in a chair, eyes closed and face set in a dreamy smile. She felt relieved. This highest state of bliss could only be caused by food.

Elizabeth was right. Mr. Pollack's experiment sat on the round pine table. It was a cake they had learned to make in Germany, a golden brown *Apfelkuchen* covered with apple slices and powdered sugar.

After two pieces of cake, Elizabeth and Jonathan were ready to discuss the mystery. Elizabeth watched her father's face as she read the notes from the interview with Uncle Rudy. She could always count on her father to bring her down to earth. "The coins haven't been seen in almost forty years?" He had a way of raising his eyebrows until they looked like two question marks. "Well, that's quite a . . . challenge. And as for the curse . . ." He turned to Elizabeth. "I'm sure you don't believe in such superstitions."

"I know, Dad. It's not scientific." She decided not to bring up the subject of the man in the blue parka.

Early the next morning Elizabeth pounded on the wall separating her bedroom from Jonathan's. "The meeting of the Pollack Detective Agency will now come to order." Soon the two were settled in her room. They sat on the floor in a patch of sunlight, with the red detective notebook between them. Fritzi, their bright green parakeet, sat in his cage in the corner. As soon as he saw Jonathan, he rang his bell and ran back and forth on his perch.

"Sorry, Fritzi," said Elizabeth. "You can't come out when we're having a meeting. You know you always get in trouble."

Fritzi stretched his neck. His chirping and clicking gradually formed into words. "Dust mites." The parakeet's words were soft, but crystal clear. "You're all dirty. Dust mites."

Elizabeth narrowed her eyes at Jonathan. "Dust mites?"

"Yep. I'm improving his vocabulary. I'm teaching Fritzi all about *The Encyclopedia of the Totally Disgusting.*"

This time Elizabeth couldn't hide her grimace. A talking parakeet with the vocabulary of her eight-year-old brother. She tossed her head, as if she could shake the thought from her mind.

"Anyway, we need to discuss something. Mom says there's a new professor in her department at the college. She teaches ancient history, or something, and she might know about old coins. So we need to make an appointment to see her."

"I know," said Jonathan. "We're supposed to get background information. Just like it says in your stupid . . . in your detective handbook."

Elizabeth chose to ignore his remark. She brought in the telephone from the hallway and stared at the receiver. She hated making calls to grown-ups she didn't know. She swallowed hard, trying to keep her mouth from turning to chalk dust. "Just sit there and be quiet while I talk. I have to concentrate."

As Elizabeth dialed the number, she heard Jonathan humming sweetly. Too sweetly. When his face drooped into an innocent puppy-eyed look, she knew she was in trouble. Still humming, Jonathan crawled across the floor and slid open the door to Fritzi's cage. An instant later the parakeet was perched on Elizabeth's shoulder, stretching his neck to get a nibble at the telephone receiver.

"Jonathan," hissed Elizabeth. She was about to hang up, but already the secretary's crisp voice was on the line. "Department of History. May I help you?"

"You're all dirty," announced Fritzi. "All dirty." Elizabeth hadn't even had a chance to speak. "I love you," cooed Fritzi. "Idiot."

"Hello. This is the Department of History." The voice wasn't quite so bright this time.

"Hi . . uh. This is Mrs. . . . , I mean, Professor Pollack's daughter." Elizabeth kept her mouth close to the receiver, glaring at Jonathan as she tried to shake Fritzi off her shoulder. The bird was in a talking mood and back on the subject of dust mites.

When Elizabeth finished talking, she deposited Fritzi in his cage. "Jonathan, you're fired." She stomped out of the room and down the stairs. It was ten minutes before she could be coaxed into talking.

"Oh, all right. The person we want to see is named Professor O'Connell. Just about everyone is gone because of winter vacation, but she'll be there this afternoon. She has an office right down the hall from Mom's. We can go any time we want, and Mom says we have to walk." Elizabeth and Jonathan couldn't complain. Milton College was only a few blocks away. Elizabeth could see the slender brick bell tower from her bedroom window.

They set out just after lunch, under a gray sky swollen with snow. The college seemed strange and lonely without the students, like a big old empty house. Not a single person was in sight as they made their way across the deserted streets and wide sidewalks. To Elizabeth, even Jonathan's constant chatter was welcome. Anything to break the icy stillness of the campus. They headed toward a long, red brick building, one of three set importantly around a large stone fountain. Jonathan opened the door and sent a few dry leaves scurrying into the hallway.

Lincoln Hall was a wheezy old place, the setting of several campus ghost stories. Elizabeth could see why. Without the lively crowd of students, the building seemed to take on a life of its own. The wooden floors creaked, complaining of their age; the fluorescent lights hummed; the ancient radiators sputtered and hissed. Elizabeth led the way down a long hallway, walking quickly past a dim alcove with a life-sized wax figure of Abraham Lincoln.

Their mother's office, like the others, was empty and dark. The secretary had left for the day, and a single shaft of light came from an open door at the end of the hall.

"That must be Professor O'Connell's office," whispered Elizabeth. "Here's what we'll do. I made the phone call, so when we get to her office, it's your turn to do the talking. Just don't talk too fast. You know how you get when you're nervous."

Elizabeth read the sign next to the open door. *Marian O'Connell, Assistant Professor of History.* They stood in the doorway uncertainly. Inside, a young woman sat in the middle of the floor among messy piles of books and papers. She was wearing a jogging suit, and her hair was tied back carelessly in a long ponytail.

"Excuse me, we're looking for Professor O'Connell," said Elizabeth softly.

The young woman stood up and smiled. "Then you've come to the right place. I'm Professor O'Connell. And you must be the children who are interested in ancient coins."

She moved a pile of books and uncovered two wooden chairs. "Sorry about the mess. I'm new here, so I'm just moving in." She tucked a wisp of stray hair behind her ear and sat down on a chair opposite theirs. "So what can I do for you?"

Elizabeth nodded to Jonathan. He was fidgeting with his mittens and had to be prodded with a light kick.

"Okay. Right." Jonathan started slowly, like a steam engine chugging out of a station, but he soon began to gain speed. "Well, see, there's this man, and his name is Uncle Rudy, only he's not our real uncle, just a friend of the family. He's pretty old, except he doesn't look old because he's so tall and he sprays black stuff on his hair so you don't see the gray." Jonathan took a gulp of air as he worked himself up to full throttle. "And actually he's a millionaire, but he still eats peanut butter and jelly sandwiches for lunch. And when we go to Milwaukee he's going to pay for us to stay at a fancy hotel, and we get to order things from room service, but I've never had room service, so I don't know if they have anything good, and . . . uh . . . uh." Jonathan sputtered to a stop, lost in his own story. Professor O'Connell was staring at him, completely mystified. "And he asked us to help him find some old coins that were lost a long time ago," Jonathan added quickly.

Professor O'Connell nodded, looking relieved. "Ah, the coins."

"You see, we're training to be detectives," said Elizabeth. She tried to will herself not to blush, but she could feel a bloom of warmth spreading across her face. "And we're trying to find five gold coins, probably Roman coins, that have been missing for forty years. My detective handbook," at this point she gave Jonathan a glare of warning, "says it's important to have background information, so we're trying to find out more about the coins."

"Well. This sounds very intriguing," said Professor O'Connell. "Why don't you tell me what you know about the coins, and I'll see if I can help you?"

Elizabeth opened her notebook. "Let's see. There are five coins, and they were found in 1789 by a farmer—a German farmer near a town called Graberstadt. They're made of gold, about the size of a dime. Some just have designs, and some have the head of a bird carved on them."

"And they're not flat," added Jonathan. "They're like little saucers. Uncle Rudy's father called them rainbow cup coins."

"Rainbow cup coins?" Professor O'Connell broke out in a wide smile. "Well, that's wonderful, just wonderful."

She climbed up on her chair and took down a fat volume from the top shelf of her bookcase. "Oh, yes. I can tell you about rainbow cup coins." She sat on the edge of her chair with the huge volume balanced on her knees.

"You mean *rainbow cup coins* is the real name?" asked Elizabeth.

"Well, it's a translation. Most historians use the German word. A lovely, long word. *Regenbogenschuesselchen.* The coins are very distinctive because they're always made of gold and shaped like little saucers. The rainbow part of the name comes from a superstition that the coins were made at the end of the rainbow."

"So, are they Roman coins?" asked Elizabeth.

"No, not Roman. Rainbow cup coins were made by the Celtic people. They lived in Bavaria before the Romans conquered that area, even before the Germanic tribes invaded."

Jonathan jumped off his chair and began dribbling an imaginary basketball. "Those Celtic people who made the coins. Is that the same word as the Boston Celtics?" He looked at Professor O'Connell, ignoring Elizabeth's grimace.

"Actually, it is," she laughed. "Quite a few Irish people settled in Boston, and Ireland is one of the few places where the Celtic people have survived. Some people there even speak the old Celtic language." She pointed to a row of cassette tapes. "You see, that's my special interest. There aren't many people who use Irish as their everyday language any more. I spend my summers in Ireland, making tapes of people who still speak in the old way."

Another memory keeper, thought Elizabeth. She and Jonathan seemed to be going from one to the next. "So the rainbow cup coins—do you know how old they are?"

Professor O'Connell ran her finger along a chart in her book. "Let's see. Rainbow cup coins were made between the third and first centuries B.C. So I would say the coins you're looking for are at least two thousand years old."

"Two thousand years old?" shouted Jonathan. "Then I bet they must be worth a lot of money."

"Well . . . possibly." Professor O'Connell tapped her fingers together and gazed out the window, as if she were deciding whether or not to say something.

"There's one more thing you should know about rainbow cup coins," she said. "I'm not trying to scare you, but I need to warn you about something. If you do find the coins, you'll need to be very careful."

Elizabeth felt her stomach do a somersault. Please, not another curse.

Professor O'Connell sat down at her computer. "I saw a newspaper article on the Web the other day. I'm sure I saved it. Here. I'll print it for you."

Jonathan and Elizabeth sat silently as the printer gave out a high-pitched whine. Professor O'Connell pulled a sheet of paper out of the machine and handed it to Elizabeth.

As Elizabeth read the title, she felt her heart take off at a gallop. *Rainbow Cup Coins Disappearing from Collections Worldwide. Twenty Thefts Reported in Last Six Months.*

Staying on the Case

Elizabeth quickly skimmed the article, trying to make sense of the strange facts she was reading. Twenty thefts of rainbow cup coins in the last six months. Police suspect an international theft ring. Most coins stolen from Europe and United States. No suspects. No arrests. Museums and private collectors urged to take precautions. She handed the paper to Jonathan, whose only reaction was an enthusiastic "Oh, cool!"

"I don't get it," said Elizabeth. "How come people are stealing rainbow cup coins all of a sudden?"

"No one knows for sure," said Professor O'Connell. "But my guess is there's a wealthy collector somewhere in the world who's suddenly taken an interest in collecting rainbow cup coins. And whoever it is must be paying top dollar. Some of the thefts have been quite daring. The thieves are going to great lengths to get hold of rainbow cup coins."

Elizabeth sat with her hands tightly folded. What if she and Jonathan weren't the only ones looking for Uncle Rudy's lost coins?

"I hope I haven't upset you," added Professor O'Connell. "I certainly don't think you have anything to worry about. But just to be on the safe side, I wouldn't broadcast the fact that you're looking for rainbow cup coins. And if you do find them, they should be put in a safe place right away."

Elizabeth and Jonathan gathered up their things and said good-bye to the professor. They walked silently down the dim hallway. Jonathan stopped to admire a display of Iron Age spearheads, but Elizabeth pulled him away and sat him down on a bench at the end of the hall.

"Jonathan, listen. There's something I'm worried about. Ever since Uncle Rudy asked us to find those coins, I've had this feeling we're being watched. First there was that man in the blue parka writing down our license number. And then I saw a man in the same color coat down the street from Mr. Lattimore's shop. As soon as I came out, he turned around and rushed into a store."

"Why would someone want to watch us?" asked Jonathan. He had gotten up and was slowly edging his way back toward the display case.

"Don't you get it? What if some people found out we're looking for rainbow cup coins? They could be watching us so they can steal the coins when we find them."

"But how could anyone know we're looking for rainbow cup coins?" Jonathan pranced up and down the hallway, making thrusts with an imaginary sword. "If you ask me, you're just being weird."

"Well, I don't care what you think. I'm the one who saw that man in the blue parka, and I think there's something strange going on. I can feel it."

Elizabeth jumped slightly as the heavy outside door swung open. She turned to see her mother walking into the hallway, her coat glistening with snow.

"I'm glad you kids are done. It's wonderful outside. I was just out walking." She brushed a shower of snow off her shoulders. "So how did your interview go?"

"It was really cool, Mom," said Jonathan. "Professor O'Connell told us all kinds of things about Uncle Rudy's coins. They're two thousand years old, and rainbow cup coins is their real name, and the Romans didn't make them, but the Celtic people did. Anyway, and then we found out that some gang of thieves is stealing rainbow cup coins all over the place. And there's that man who was writing down our license number at Uncle Rudy's. Elizabeth thinks he's one of the thieves and he's watching us so he can steal the coins as soon as we find them."

"I think you'll have to run that by me again when we get back," said Mrs. Pollack slowly.

By the time they reached home, the air was thick with snow. The three stomped into the house and hung their wet coats by the heating vent. As they settled themselves in the living room, Mr. Pollack walked out of his study and joined them. Elizabeth went over the story again.

"That does sound strange," said Mr. Pollack thoughtfully. "Especially the part about the man copying down our license number. But there's no way he could have anything to do with the coin thieves. How could any thieves have found out that you're looking for rainbow cup coins?"

"I don't know. I just have this *feeling*. What do you think, Mom?"

"Well . . . I think it's important for a detective to have imagination, but sometimes, Elizabeth, your imagination gets a little too active."

"Yeah, and Pop always says not to dwell on things," said Jonathan.

Elizabeth tried to follow Pop's advice. Upstairs in her room, she grabbed a book and flopped down on her bed. Fritzi rang his bell twice, hoping for a greeting. Elizabeth stared at the book for a moment, then set it aside and leaned over to Fritzi's cage. "I know everyone thinks I'm crazy," she said, "but there's something strange going on. I just know it." Fritzi cocked his head and gave her a beady-eyed stare. "Dust mites," he cooed softly. "You're all dirty."

Elizabeth's dark mood didn't last long. The day was simply too perfect—five inches of snow, roast chicken and dumplings for dinner, and a lively card game in the evening. And yet she couldn't quite forget the coin thefts and the suspicious man in the blue parka.

At five minutes before nine, Elizabeth suddenly pushed her chair back and slapped her cards down on the table. "I've got to do something. I'll be back in a few minutes." She rushed away from the kitchen table and disappeared up the stairs. In a few minutes she was back, holding a sheet of paper in her hand.

"I think we should all go in the living room," she said. "There's something we need to talk about."

Elizabeth remained standing as the others sat on the couch. "I just talked to Uncle Rudy on the phone." She knew this wasn't going to please her mother. "I know I should have asked first, Mom, but I just had to talk to Uncle Rudy. I needed to find out if he told anyone else about the rainbow cup coins. Or if he told anyone Jonathan and I are helping him."

"Well?" asked Mr. Pollack. "Don't keep us in suspense. Did he tell anyone?"

"I'll say he did. He put an ad in the newspaper. About the coins."

"An ad in the newspaper?" repeated Jonathan. "Why would he do that?"

"This was a few weeks ago. He thought maybe he could find someone who knew what happened to the coins. He read the ad to me just now and I wrote it down." Elizabeth looked at the sheet in her hand. "Listen to this: *Seeking information on missing coins. Description: five gold coins, saucer-shaped, known as rainbow cup coins, last seen thirty-nine years ago at the King's Home for Retired Gentlemen. Reward for information. No questions asked. Contact Rudolf Obermeyer, 877-4236.*"

"So what happened?" asked Mrs. Pollack.

"He didn't get any calls. That's probably why he didn't tell us about the ad. But some coin thief could have seen the ad in the paper and found out where Uncle Rudy lives. Maybe he's watching to see if the coins are found, so he can steal them. And then he figured out that we're helping Uncle Rudy, so he's spying on us too."

"Let me get this straight," said Mr. Pollack. "You think the man in the blue parka, the one who wrote down our license number, is a coin thief who saw the ad in the paper. Somehow he found out that you two are helping Uncle Rudy find the coins, so now he's following you, waiting to see if you find them."

Elizabeth slouched into an armchair. "I don't know what I think. I guess it does sound pretty ridiculous. But it's possible. Uncle Rudy said he did tell a lot of people we were coming to help him. And with that booming voice of his, anyone could have overheard him."

Mrs. Pollack stood up. "Look, I don't like the way this is going. First the old diary talks about curses and danger. And now you find out about coin thieves and tell me you think someone's been watching you. I don't know. This just hasn't turned out the way we expected."

Elizabeth stared down at the smooth blue carpet. She knew she was going to hear something she wouldn't like. She felt her mother's hand lightly touch her shoulder. "I think you and Jonathan should give up this case. I'm sure Uncle Rudy would understand. You're just kids. You're supposed to be having fun, not worrying about things like this."

"No way, Mom," said Elizabeth. "We're not giving up the case. We promised Uncle Rudy we would help him. And Jonathan and I really do want to be detectives. Not just pretend ones either." She shrugged her shoulders. "Maybe it's not so good to gather too much information. I mean, that man in the parking garage—he probably just worked there or something." She was trying hard to convince herself.

"Well, anyway, I'm not afraid of any coin thieves," said Jonathan. He picked up a ball-point pen and struck a threatening pose, adding a dramatic karate kick which sent him crashing to the floor.

"See, Mom. Jonathan will protect me."

"I'll tell you what," said Mr. Pollack. "I don't think there are any coin thieves hot on your trail, but I'm going to call Uncle Rudy back right now. I'll ask him not to mention to anyone outside the family when we're coming to Milwaukee or where we're going to be staying. We'll just have to be extra careful from now on."

Elizabeth sneaked a look at her mother's face. She wasn't saying anything, so that meant she agreed. Somehow everyone did seem to feel better. Before she went to bed, Elizabeth checked the things-to-do list in her detective notebook. There was nothing more to be done on the case except wait for spring vacation. Elizabeth slid open the top drawer of her desk and carefully put her red notebook away.

With each passing week, the thoughts of danger and curses and coin thieves became fainter. By the time spring vacation approached, no one had time to think about the trip to Milwaukee. Jonathan worried over his role as a singing tomato in the second grade musical, and Elizabeth was up until midnight measuring radish sprouts for her science fair project. After the last day of school, she burst in the front door, kicked off her shoes, and flopped down on the couch.

"Do me a favor, Mom, and don't wake me up for about three days."

"Don't worry," laughed Mrs. Pollack. "You'll have plenty of time to rest. We're not going to Milwaukee until Monday."

"And what about Dad?" asked Elizabeth.

"He'll take the train up on Tuesday night. After the Science Club field trip."

Elizabeth spent a lazy Saturday and waited until Sunday afternoon to begin packing. After zipping her suitcase shut, she called Jonathan into her room.

"I think we'd better look over our case notes. We want to be ready for tomorrow." She opened her detective notebook and skimmed the first page. "Okay. Here's the main clue. Rudy's father said, *The coins are in a safe place. I'll have to show you the hidden key.* So when we search that old furniture, we should be looking for the coins or maybe just the key."

Elizabeth read the notes out loud to Jonathan, going over all the information they had gathered. For months, there had been little time to think about the missing coins. Now, page by page, the mystery came back into focus, like a shadowy figure slowly stepping into the light.

When they finished, Elizabeth closed her detective notebook and ran her hand over the shiny red cover. She glanced at her suitcase, packed and ready to go. She and Jonathan looked at each other. They didn't say a word, but they both had the same feeling. Something important was about to happen.

Before she went to bed that night, Elizabeth read through her notebook one more time. She could picture everything. Uncle Rudy, business-like and booming with optimism. The old diary, filled with his grandmother's strange and beautiful handwriting. And finally Mr. Kruger, slowly and hesitantly translating the words that had held them spellbound. *"If the coins are lost, they must be found before forty years have passed. If not, a great misfortune will befall the family. But once the coins are lost, finding them will be difficult, very difficult. It is said they can only be found by a person with a heart that dares to face danger."*

Elizabeth closed the notebook softly and turned off the light. Somehow she was no longer frightened by the strange words or worried by thoughts of coin thieves. Only one thing was important now. Finally, after months of waiting, their investigation would be starting for real. At this very moment, the five ancient coins were waiting, hidden in some quiet and secret place. And the path to that place, Elizabeth felt, would not be straight, but full of twists and turns.

Expect the Unexpected

9:05 AM We're on the road, heading north. Day is cold and blustery. Elizabeth leaned away from Jonathan and hunched over her journal as she wrote. *I hid THE BOOK under a pile of bath towels. Best hiding place ever. Jonathan won't find it for months. Maybe even years.* Elizabeth looked up and gazed at her brother. He was actually reading a book other than *The Encyclopedia of the Totally Disgusting.* A nice normal chapter book about a boy and his dog. Finally. A trip without lectures on boils, blood blisters, or the making of a scab. Elizabeth rewarded Jonathan with a pat on the head and an encouraging smile. He narrowed his eyes suspiciously and stuck out his tongue. Elizabeth checked her watch. Twenty minutes down and five hours to go.

It was early afternoon and well north of Chicago before Elizabeth spotted what she had been longing for—a distant gray outline of tall buildings and delicate church spires. As soon as Mrs. Pollack turned off the expressway, Milwaukee closed in on them with a maze of crowded city streets.

"If I'm reading the map right," said Mrs. Pollack, "our hotel should be right around this corner." As she spoke, a stately brick building came into view. Mrs. Pollack pulled the car up to the entrance, magically unleashing a flurry of activity. Two men in maroon and black uniforms appeared out of nowhere. As one unloaded the suitcases and carried them inside, the other took charge of the car.

Elizabeth plunged into a revolving door, hurried along by a gritty gust of March wind. Behind her, Jonathan pushed the door hard and sent them both half tumbling into the lobby. Elizabeth glanced around uncertainly, as if she had been swept into some strange, faraway place. The Edwardian Hotel was a world of its own, tucked into the heart of the city like a warm, golden secret. It was . . . Elizabeth thought back to last week's spelling list. It was *splendorous.* Marble. Polished wood. Glowing chandeliers. And from some-where, the sound of violin music danced sweetly through the air.

Elizabeth saw her mother pass by, but she didn't follow. She leaned her head back to study the distant ceiling, where golden cherubs drifted among painted clouds. "Wow," she whispered. "I feel like Dorothy walking into the Emerald City."

Jonathan gave her a nudge. "Yeah, and there's Toto." An elegant young woman glided by, carrying a tiny black puff of a dog done up in pink bows.

Elizabeth and Jonathan hurried to catch up with Mrs. Pollack and stood beside her at the registration desk. Behind the counter stood a small, tidy man, his dark hair slicked back as sleek as an otter. He took off his reading glasses and gazed at them with a polite smile. Elizabeth pulled her ponytail tight and stood close to the desk, glad that her sneakers and wrinkled blue jeans were out of sight.

"We're the Pollack family," announced her mother. "We have reservations arranged by Mr. Obermeyer."

The man's smile widened as he stepped out from behind the desk. "Oh, yes. Yes, of course. We've been expecting you. The brilliant detectives." Elizabeth glanced around uneasily. She wished he hadn't said it quite so loudly. "Allow me to introduce myself," said the man, bowing slightly. "E. Postlethwaite-Brown, Desk Man-ager, at your service. You may call me Mr. P."

He pulled at his cuff and smoothed out an invisible wrinkle in his sleeve. "Mr. Obermeyer has spoken to me personally about your accommodations. You are to have a three-room suite on the twentieth floor. He wishes you to avail yourselves of our excellent room service at any time, day or night. At his expense, of course. And you need not worry about gratuities. Mr. Obermeyer will take care of compensating the staff."

Jonathan's mouth fell open wider at every word. Mrs. Pollack whispered a translation. "That means we can use room service as much as we want, and we don't have to pay any tips."

As Mr. P gave a barely perceptible nod, another uniformed man appeared. "Our luggage attendant will bring your bags to the room. And if you would follow me, please, I'll show you the way to the elevator. The guests staying in our suites have an elevator for their exclusive use."

Mr. P strode across the lobby. With one arm extended, he cleared a path for them as if they were visiting royalty. The three giggled their way up the elevator to the twentieth floor.

"Oh, I don't know," laughed Mrs. Pollack. "I'm not used to all this luxury."

They walked down an empty hallway and found their suite, with the door open and their luggage placed inside.

Elizabeth tiptoed into a large sitting room done up in quiet tones of burgundy and gold. It was definitely not a flop-down, feet-on-the-coffee-table place. The sofas and chairs were straight-backed and trim, the kind of furniture that would have a British accent if it could talk. Elizabeth could see two elegant bedrooms opening up on either side of the room.

Jonathan lost no time in taking possession. First he made a dive for a bowl of mints on the coffee table. Then he tested the couch cushions, punched a few buttons on the television, opened and closed the curtains twice, and accidentally turned on the air conditioner. Elizabeth half expected an alarm to ring and Mr. P to hustle them out of the hotel.

"I'll call Uncle Rudy and Aunt Lorraine," said Mrs. Pollack, "to tell them we're here. You keep an eye on Jonathan. Something tells me he could get into trouble."

Elizabeth watched Jonathan disappear into an immense marble bathroom. She waited for a few minutes, but Jonathan didn't come out. When she heard the bath water running she rushed to the door. If Jonathan was willingly taking a bath, something was wrong. Very wrong.

"What are you doing in there?"

"Jacuzzi!" cried Jonathan. He had to yell over the roar of water. "You should see how fast the water comes out. And there's lots of other neat stuff." A few seconds later, a strong pine scent drifted out. Elizabeth rolled her eyes, wondering if the Edwardian Hotel would survive three days of Jonathan Pollack.

"Jon, open up." She jiggled the door knob.

"Aromatherapy!" called Jonathan. "They have little nozzles in the wall and different smells come out. I think it's supposed to give you more energy."

Jonathan with more energy? Elizabeth's eyes widened in horror. She scurried into the sitting room. "Mom! Jonathan's locked in the bathroom with the Jacuzzi and something called aromatherapy." Mrs. Pollack hung up the phone and ordered Jonathan to open the door. As soon as the Jacuzzi was turned off, Jonathan was hustled out of the bathroom under protest.

"Getting back to the *mystery*," said Mrs. Pollack, "I just talked to Uncle Rudy. Here's the plan. His daughter Zina took the afternoon off from work, so we can go to her house as soon as we're ready. She lives on the East Side, not very far from here. I said we'd take the bus."

"The bus?" crowed Jonathan. Elizabeth gave him a jab of warning. Their mother could be a bit like Pop sometimes. If they argued, they were sure to get a long lecture on the benefits of public transportation.

"That's right," said Mrs. Pollack. "You know what I always say."

"Yeah," said Jonathan. "You don't really get to know a city unless you take the bus."

"Exactly. I called the desk and got all the information from Mr. P. The bus stops right in front of the hotel, and it's only about a ten-minute ride to Zina's house. She wants to take us out to dinner later, so she'll give us a ride back."

A few minutes later, the three were seated on the long front seat of a city bus. Elizabeth swung her backpack onto her lap and pressed her hands on her knees. Now that their investigation was starting for real, nothing could stop the jittery feeling that made her legs want to jiggle up and down. She sat up straight, reminding herself that she was Elizabeth Pollack, ace detective. It was no use. She felt more like Cinderella at two minutes after midnight. The ace detective had turned back into an eleven-year-old girl with skinny legs, a droopy ponytail, and a pesky kid brother.

She started slightly when Mrs. Pollack touched her arm. "You know, I was just thinking about Zina. I haven't seen her in so many years. I wonder if she's changed."

"Changed?"

"Well, she used to be pretty wild, and a great one for practical jokes. Of course, she's older now and has grown children. And I think she's a lawyer. Anyway, maybe she's gotten more serious. But if I were you, I'd expect the unexpected. Just think of Aunt Marie, but multiplied by five."

Elizabeth looked at her mother doubtfully. Aunt Marie was Mrs. Pollack's sister. The one who kept a plastic arm in the trunk of her car and had four fright wigs and a set of fake teeth. She couldn't imagine Aunt Marie multiplied by five.

After the driver called out their stop, they stepped off the bus quickly and found the small side street where Zina lived. About halfway down the block, Mrs. Pollack stopped in front of a massive old house of cream-colored brick, sitting close to the sidewalk.

Elizabeth liked the place immediately, with its long, narrow windows and gingerbread woodwork curling over the porch. She didn't know why, but she had the strangest feeling the house was smiling.

Jonathan pushed past the others and ran up the front steps. A moment later, a loud noise burst forth from the porch. Elizabeth drew back in disgust.

"Jonathan!" cried Mrs. Pollack. "How dare you!" There was no mistaking what they had heard—the longest, loudest, most king-sized belch ever produced.

Jonathan shook his head vigorously. "Mom, it wasn't me. It was . . . Well, I think it was . . . the doorbell. Here, I'll show you." As Elizabeth and Mrs. Pollack stepped onto the porch, he pressed a small white button, producing a second, identical belch.

Before they had quite recovered, the door was swung open by a tall woman with dark curls tumbling down to her shoulders. Uncle Rudy's daughter stood before them, dressed in overalls and carrying a spear-like object with a rag over the tip. Zina stepped out and swept Mrs. Pollack into an enthusiastic embrace.

"Amanda," she boomed. "It's so good to see you." She greeted Jonathan and Elizabeth with energetic handshakes, then put down the spear—Elizabeth could see now that it was a broom handle. "Come on in. I was just clearing out cobwebs from the attic."

The two stepped in cautiously behind their mother. "I like that burping doorbell," ventured Jonathan.

"I know! Isn't it great? My kids gave it to me for Christmas. So now I don't have any trouble with people selling things door-to-door." As Zina smiled, her eyes narrowed into two slits of pure mischief. Jonathan gazed at her in awe.

After Zina helped them with their coats, she rubbed her hands together. "Well, I'm sure you two would rather start working than listen to us gabbing. Dad says you want to take a look at Grandpa's furniture. It's all up in the attic. I hope you don't mind working up there." The four of them tapped up a wooden stairway, then down a long hallway. The last door was painted black. Elizabeth looked up at the crude letters chalked on the door. *Abandon hope, all ye who enter here.*

"My kids are grown up now," said Zina, "but they always used to play in the attic." She gazed up lovingly at the words. "Don't worry though. I think we've gotten rid of all the booby traps." She led them up a narrow staircase to a roomy attic. It was the kind of place Elizabeth had always wished for—a storybook attic full of trunks and boxes and strange bulky shapes covered with sheets. Elizabeth's eyes were drawn to the opposite corner, which was lit by an eerie orange glow.

"I turned on the space heater a little while ago so you won't freeze," said Zina. She clicked on a small light bulb and led them to a corner of the attic. "Here it is. My grandfather's furniture." She pulled away two large white sheets, revealing a desk, a dresser, and two wide bookcases.

"But . . . is this everything?" Elizabeth pressed her lips together. She had expected more. Much more.

"That's right. These are the only pieces Grandpa Obermeyer brought with him when he moved into the King's Home." She ran her hand over the smooth dark wood of the old dresser. "It's too bad. I just never found a place for them downstairs."

Zina opened the top drawer of the dresser. "Oh, and don't be startled if you find a few strange little items in the drawers. My kids used to store their treasures up here." She pulled out a long rubber snake and a fake spider as big as her hand.

"Don't worry," said Jonathan. "We know every trick in the book."

Zina nodded and turned to leave. "Well, we'll leave you two to your work. Your mom and I will be down in the living room if you need us."

Jonathan peered into a dark corner. "Uh, what's that?"

"Oh, sorry. I forgot to introduce you to Mr. B." Zina walked into the corner and wheeled out a life-sized skeleton dangling limply from a metal frame. "Don't worry. He's just plastic. I used to be a biology teacher before I went to law school." She gave the skull an affectionate pat.

Mrs. Pollack bent down next to Jonathan. "You sure you'll be all right alone up here? It is a little spooky."

"Mom, we're not babies," said Elizabeth. "It's no big deal. We're fine." She unzipped her backpack as her mother and Zina walked down the stairs.

"Okay, Jon. Now first we have to—"

"It's alive!" shouted Jonathan. "Abandon ship, matey!" He grabbed Elizabeth's arm and half dragged her down the stairs. They caught up with Mrs. Pollack and Zina in the hallway.

"I thought it was a joke," he said breathlessly. "So I walked towards it, and then it started moving."

Zina led the way back up the stairs to the attic. Standing next to Mrs. Pollack in the safety of the doorway, Jonathan pointed to a dark shape on the floor behind the dresser. Zina walked over and stood over the object of his terror. It was a rat—squirming, gray, and enormously fat.

"So that's where you've been," said Zina. She picked up the rat and cradled it tenderly in her arms. "I'm certainly glad you found Chucky," she said brightly. "I've been looking for him for weeks."

Looking for Secrets

Zina turned the rat over and pressed its stomach. The squirming stopped.

"Sorry it scared you, Jonathan, but you were right. It is just a fake. When someone walks nearby, the vibrations make the power turn on and the rat starts moving." She shook her head at Chucky. "I don't know how he got up here. I usually keep him under a chair in the guest bedroom."

"Uh . . . another gift from your kids?" asked Elizabeth.

"Birthday present," said Zina. "Those kids really know what I like." She held out the rat and let Jonathan have a close-up look. "Do you want me to leave him up here to keep you company?"

"That's okay," said Elizabeth. "We'll be fine without him." She stood at the top of the stairs, watching Zina walk down behind Mrs. Pollack. A burping doorbell. A skeleton in the attic. A high tech fake rat. The Obermeyers weren't exactly the average American family.

"You know, Jonathan, I think we just learned something."

Jonathan nodded his head reverently. "Yeah. As soon as I get that reward money, I'm gonna buy a rat just like Chucky."

"Not about that. I mean we learned that the Obermeyers don't do things like most people do. I'm sure Uncle Rudy's father wanted him to have the coins. But somehow I have a feeling he didn't keep them in the kind of place most people would."

"Oh, well, who cares?" said Jonathan. "Let's just start looking."

Elizabeth unpacked her backpack and took stock of their tools: two flashlights, two rulers, one detective notebook, and a magnifying glass. They started with the bookcases, turning them upside down and examining every inch of the dark wood. Elizabeth wasn't surprised that the plain, solid shelves hid no secrets.

Jonathan trained his flashlight on the desk. It was a simple piece, with a long middle drawer and three smaller drawers on either side. It didn't look the slightest bit mysterious, or even very old. Elizabeth had the same kind of hand-me-down desk in her own room. Almost every family she knew had one too.

"I don't know about this one, but let's give it a try." Elizabeth removed each drawer, inspecting it closely and measuring the depth. Jonathan investigated the shell of the desk. After a few minutes' work, they traded jobs and inspected the desk again. Elizabeth replaced the drawers and stood up. They had found nothing interesting.

Elizabeth turned to the last piece of furniture, a delicate old dresser. The warm brown wood glowed reddish in the light of the space heater. The front was covered with carving and fancy woodwork.

"Now this looks promising," said Elizabeth. She ran her hands along the front of the drawers, each with a keyhole surrounded by elaborate carving. "Remember when we interviewed Mr. Lattimore? He told us that sometimes things look like decoration, but they're really springs. And they make secret compartments open up." They examined each piece of woodwork with the magnifying glass, pushing and twisting and turning. Not one piece budged.

The two worked together to remove three heavy, deep drawers. Again they discovered nothing, either in the drawers or in the dresser itself. After replacing the large drawers, they pulled out two long, narrow handkerchief drawers at the top of the dresser.

Elizabeth grabbed her ruler. "Mine's three and a half inches deep," she said.

"Mine's just three."

Jonathan's words sent Elizabeth into action. She picked up the drawer and rushed over to the window, where the light was better. She could see right away that the drawer in her hand wasn't quite as deep as the other.

"Jonathan, can't you ever be serious?" She shook Mr. B's skeleton hand from her shoulder, where her brother had placed it. As Jonathan looked on, she turned the drawer sideways then upside down. As she did so, the back panel of the drawer slid out and clattered to the floor. Elizabeth held her breath. There was a dark opening, a space about half an inch high and three inches wide, between the false bottom and the real bottom of the drawer. Plenty of space for a hidden key. Or for five ancient gold coins.

Slowly, Elizabeth tipped the drawer and held out her hand. She closed her eyes, sure that she would soon feel the five gold coins clink into her palm. She popped open her eyes as she felt something touch her hand lightly. It was a small, white piece of paper, folded in half.

As Elizabeth unfolded the note, she saw two lines of bold capital letters. Their message seemed to fly out at her, like an arrow hitting its mark. DON'T FORGET THE HIDDEN KEY. IT LEADS TO A GARDEN OF THREE. Elizabeth edged away from the skeleton as she read the words again. She remembered the last case they worked on, when a long lost note brought a piece of the past to life. And now she felt the same chill, as if a voice from long ago had traveled over time and whispered in her ear.

"Uncle Rudy's father must have written this," she said, handing the note to Jonathan. "But what does he mean—*a garden of three?*"

"I don't get it either. But maybe Zina knows something about —"

"Did I hear my name?" Zina's voice burst up from the bottom of the stairs. "We were just coming up to see how you're doing."

"We found a secret compartment!" shouted Jonathan. "And a clue!"

Zina pounded up the stairs, with Mrs. Pollack behind her. Elizabeth showed them the secret compartment, and Jonathan held up the note.

"*Don't forget the hidden key,*" read Mrs. Pollack. *"It leads to a garden of three."* She looked at Zina. "A garden of three?"

Zina shook her head. "It's a great clue, but unfortunately I have no idea what it means. Grandma and Grandpa always lived in apartments. They never even had a garden." She took the drawer from Elizabeth and peered into the hidden opening. "I never knew about this secret compartment. I'll tell you one thing. My father's going to be excited about this. And he might be able to make some sense out of that note."

Elizabeth waited in the living room with Jonathan and Mrs. Pollack as Zina called her father.

"It's all set," said Zina. "Mom's not feeling too well tonight, but Dad wants to take us all out for dinner. He says you can't visit Milwaukee without going to a German restaurant."

"I'll just change out of my overalls, then we can leave," she called over her shoulder.

Jonathan was restless, going from chair to chair like Goldilocks at the three bears' house. Elizabeth sat next to her mother on the couch, reading and rereading the note. *A garden of three.* If they could figure out that clue, they might find the coins. Even without finding the hidden key.

"You'll have to count on Uncle Rudy," said Mrs. Pollack. "He's the one person who might know what this means."

They snaked through a tangle of rush-hour traffic to get to the restaurant. Uncle Rudy's large black car pulled into the parking lot just ahead of them. Elizabeth gave Jonathan a poke and pointed out the window. A stocky young man in a suit and tie helped Uncle Rudy out of the car, then drove away. She had never seen a chauffeur before.

"A secret hiding place. Excellent work!" Uncle Rudy stood in the middle of the parking lot as they got out of the car. "I knew you were sharp ones."

He swung open the heavy wooden door. "A German restaurant on a cold day," he sighed. "Nothing better." Elizabeth stepped inside, drawn by the warm scent of spices and simmering meat. The dark-paneled walls and low ceiling gave the room a solid, cozy feel. Like a captain's cabin, thought Elizabeth, on an old sailing ship.

Uncle Rudy sat down at a round table and stretched his legs toward the warmth of a wide brick fireplace. "Now then. How about a look at that clue Zina told me about?"

Elizabeth handed him the note and studied his face as he read it. "*Don't forget the hidden key. It leads to a garden of three,*" he repeated. He set the note on the table and stared at it for a long time. "I recognize the writing," he said finally. "My father definitely wrote this. But other than that, I'm afraid I'm no help. *Garden of three.* I can't imagine what that means. What kind of garden would only have three flowers in it?" Uncle Rudy slowly folded the note and gave it back to Elizabeth. "If only I had taken the time and asked my father to tell me where he kept the coins."

"Well, there's still the King's Home," said Mrs. Pollack. "We're planning to go there tomorrow morning and take a look at the room where your father lived."

"And we'll ask about a garden," said Elizabeth. "Maybe there used to be a little garden somewhere around there."

"Excellent," said Uncle Rudy. "As usual." He picked up a menu then put it down again. "I wanted to ask you something. Your mother told me that Pop was keeping my grandmother's diary for awhile. But I was wondering, well . . ." He seemed to be choosing his words carefully. "About that page I marked in the diary."

Elizabeth looked down at the table. The diary. She had almost forgotten about it. This case was full of shadows, and they never quite went away. The old curse. The man in the blue parka. The story of the coin thefts.

"We found someone who read it to us," she said. "He told us about some kind of curse."

"So you know," said Uncle Rudy. "I wasn't sure I wanted you to find out. You see, my grandmother told me that terrible things would happen if the coins would ever be missing for more than forty years. And I suppose a sharp detective like you has figured out that the forty years is up in a few days."

Elizabeth nodded. "Exactly five days from now. All I had to do was subtract the date your father died. I had it in my notes."

"Pop said not to dwell on it," said Jonathan. He stared at the menu, which pictured a plate-sized Wiener Schnitzel and a mountain of tiny dumplings.

"Exactly," said Uncle Rudy. "No one believes that nonsense. Just don't let it bother you. No problem." His voice was softer than usual. "No problem at all."

After dinner Zina drove everyone home, stopping first at Uncle Rudy's apartment building. She pulled into the parking garage, then stopped next to the elevator and helped her father out of the car. Elizabeth leaned back against the seat, still picturing the warm Apfelstrudel she had for dessert. She turned her head and glanced out the window absentmindedly. Suddenly she slid down in her seat. Between two rows of parked cars, a man stood and stared at them. Elizabeth immediately recognized the dark hair, the coat, and the scowl. It was the man in the blue parka. The one who had written down their license number.

"Uncle Rudy," she called. "Do you know who that man is?" She turned and pointed to the end of the aisle, but the man was gone. No one else had seen him.

After returning to the hotel room that evening, Elizabeth locked the door and tested it three times. She didn't care if everyone else thought she was being silly. She was convinced that the dark-haired man, like a vulture circling overhead, was patiently waiting for them to find the rainbow cup coins.

Elizabeth fell asleep over a book and awoke to find the light still on. She started to sit up but froze as she heard gruff voices coming from the sitting room. Coins. They were saying something about the coins. She looked over at Jonathan's bed and saw it was empty. The bedroom door was slightly ajar, and through the opening she could see a man in a dark coat standing in the next room.

Elizabeth desperately lunged for the telephone on the night table. If she could just dial . . . But it was too late. The bedroom door swung wide open and a hand reached in through the doorway— the dry, white hand of a skeleton holding a squirming rat by its tail.

It must have been Elizabeth's own scream that tore her out of the nightmare. She awoke with her body tingling from head to toe, fear sparking from every pore in her body. She was too frightened to move. Turning her head, she squinted into the darkness at the red numbers on the alarm clock. 3:12 AM. A light snore sounded from Jonathan's bed. At least she hadn't screamed out loud.

Elizabeth settled down deep under the covers, forcing her thoughts away from the nightmare and back to the mystery. *The hidden key. The garden of three.* She could see the words in her mind, glaring like a neon sign. The clues had to mean something. Why couldn't she understand?

The Hidden Key

"Breakfast! You gotta see it!" Jonathan's voice came from the sitting room as he pounded on the closed bedroom door.

"Huh?" Elizabeth sat up and reached for her glasses. The curtains were still shut, letting in only a sliver of daylight.

"Hey, get up. Room service was here." Jonathan banged on the door again. Elizabeth sat up carefully, still wrapped in the covers. The ghostly visions from her nightmare were still present, lingering in the room like a faint scent. After glancing briefly into each dim corner, she counted to three, threw back the covers, and reached the door in four giant steps.

As Elizabeth plunged into the bright warmth of the sitting room, she felt her fear melt away like butter in the sun. She was never so glad to meet the morning. With the heavy curtains pulled back, the light tumbled in through the windows and painted the walls with sunshine. In the middle of the room a wheeled cart displayed their breakfast feast. Waffles, sausages, fresh fruit, granola, blueberry muffins, and steaming cups of hot chocolate. Jonathan hovered over the food, breathing deeply with folded hands. In a cartoon he would have floated into the air on waves of aroma.

Mrs. Pollack sat on the couch in her bathrobe and sipped a cup of coffee. "If this is the life of a detective," she said, "I could definitely get used to it."

An hour later the three walked out of the hotel and threaded their way among the office workers and early shoppers. Mrs. Pollack carried a city map with a red X marking the King's Home.

"Jonathan, we'll never get there if you have to kick every pile of snow. Mom's way ahead of us." Elizabeth had given up trying to understand Jonathan. He couldn't pass a stick without picking it up, and he couldn't pass a pile of anything without flattening it. She dragged him away from a rock-hard pile of dirty snow.

"Pookie McDougal puts ketchup on snow and eats it for breakfast," announced Jonathan. "And one time he made a cat food sandwich, but his mom wouldn't let him eat it." Elizabeth grimaced in silence and kept walking. Pookie McDougal, Jonathan's new friend and hero, had moved in exactly four weeks ago, striking their neighborhood like a natural disaster. He was a large-toothed ten year old with buzz-cut hair and a mind full of off-beat information. A living, breathing version of *The Encyclopedia of the Totally Disgusting*.

"You're supposed to be thinking about the rainbow cup coins, Jonathan, not cat food sandwiches."

Elizabeth picked up the pace until they caught up with their mother. Four blocks later Mrs. Pollack stopped in front of a plain-looking stone building with a double set of glass doors. As the others walked into the small lobby, Elizabeth backed up for a moment and peeked out the door. People hurried by without a glance in her direction. And no blue parkas.

Mrs. Pollack and Jonathan were already talking to a silver-haired man sitting behind a large desk. "I'm Mrs. —"

"Mrs. Pollack," said the man, as he rose from the chair. "Lou Marino. Nice to meet you. Mr. Obermeyer told me you would be coming. He said there would be some, uh, some . . . ," he looked doubtfully at Jonathan and Elizabeth, "detectives coming to look at the room where his father used to live. Follow me, please." He led them past a well-furnished lounge where a few men wearing suits and ties sat bent over newspapers. Farther down the hall, lively piano music collided with the blare of a loud television.

Mr. Marino led them up a narrow staircase to the second floor and stopped in front of a metal door marked 216.

"Before you go," said Elizabeth, "there's one more thing." She asked about the garden and received the answer she dreaded. There had never been a garden at the King's Home or anywhere nearby, not even a small one. The downtown buildings left little room for flowers. And like everyone else, Mr. Marino shook his head at the words *garden of three*. They meant nothing to him.

"You're in luck with the room though," he said as he opened the door. "This whole end of the hall is being renovated. There's nobody in here right now." They entered a small living room with a tiny bedroom attached. "You can search from top to bottom," he added as he turned to leave. "Just let me know when you're done."

Elizabeth turned slowly, looking at the empty rooms and the bare walls ready for painting. If the room had any secrets, it should be easy to find them. Jonathan stepped onto a rickety ladder with a large can of paint balanced on the top. "Pookie McDougal says people spit in their paint to make it go on smoother."

"Don't even think of it." Mrs. Pollack lifted him off the ladder.

"I was just going to *look*." Jonathan stuck out his lip in a pout, but the lure of a good search was too strong to resist. He was glad to crawl to the back of the closet or check in the cabinet underneath the bathroom sink. Elizabeth watched as he stuck his hand behind the heat vent and felt around in the dust. She gave him an encouraging smile. Once in a while Jonathan could be very useful.

They took their time, poking and pushing and peering into the tiniest places. Jonathan found a dusty coin wedged into the corner of the bedroom closet, but it turned out to be a scuffed-up 1952 penny. In less than an hour every crack and crevice had been investigated. Elizabeth's sleeves were covered with plaster dust, and Jonathan had managed to get wet paint in his hair.

Mr. Marino wasn't at the front desk when they walked down the stairs. Elizabeth wrote him a note to let him know they had left. Silently, the three walked back to the hotel and up to their suite. Their search of the rooms at the King's Home had revealed nothing. No key. No coins. Mrs. Pollack had even spoken to the painters. They hadn't found anything the least bit unusual in Room 216.

"There must be something else we can do," said Mrs. Pollack uncertainly.

"I could do the Outer Mongolian Warrior Dance," offered Jonathan. "That brings good luck."

Elizabeth winced. The Outer Mongolian Warrior Dance was Jonathan's own creation. It involved running in circles while waving a stick and grunting. The louder the better.

"Jon—forget it. You know that doesn't do any good."

"Oh, yeah? Then why don't you look in your ratty old detective book and see what it says."

"I don't have to look," said Elizabeth. "I already know what it says." She straightened up. "*How to Think Like a Detective. Chapter Six.*" Jonathan squeezed his eyes shut, but she knew he was listening. "This is called an impasse," she said. "It seems like there's nowhere to go. When that happens you're supposed to look at all the information you have. Lots of times you find out something important in the beginning, but you don't realize it until later."

Elizabeth walked over to the desk and picked up her red spiral notebook. Sitting cross-legged on the couch, she began reading her notes out loud. Jonathan sat up when she came to the part about Wilhelm Obermeyer loving to read.

"That was my question," said Jonathan. "About hobbies."

"Yeah, and I thought it was a pretty dumb thing to ask. It's more . . ." Elizabeth's voice trailed off. She slammed the notebook shut. "Books!"

Jonathan and Mrs. Pollack looked at her blankly.

"Books!" she repeated. "There were two bookcases in Zina's attic. So where are the books? That's the one thing we haven't looked at."

Mrs. Pollack picked up the telephone and handed it to Elizabeth.

"There's no reason you can't find out right now. Why don't you give Uncle Rudy a call?"

Elizabeth pressed her lips together as she listened to the ringing in the telephone. Please. He has to be home. Just as she was about to give up, Uncle Rudy's deep hello sounded. She wasted no time in getting to the all-important question. Elizabeth grabbed a pencil and wrote a few words in her notebook, then hung up the phone.

"Oh, well. I guess it could be worse. Uncle Rudy's father did have books. Lots of them. They were stored away for years and years, but no one really wanted them, so Aunt Lorraine donated them to the library. Two years ago."

"Two years ago?" asked Jonathan.

"Yeah. I know. It's not great. Anyway, I wrote down the name of the library. Uncle Rudy said it's just down the block from the King's Home. So we have to go there. Right now."

Jonathan celebrated with a few quick turns around the coffee table. What could be simpler? The key. The coins. Anything small could easily be hidden in a book.

After a quick lunch, they retraced their steps and walked toward the King's Home. They turned down a narrow side street they hadn't noticed earlier. Crowded between two tall buildings was a red brick library set back from the street.

Elizabeth ran up the wide stone steps ahead of the others. She was never shy about going into a library. It was the one place where the world seemed to slow down. And with so many books around, no one ever had to feel lonely. She waited for her mother and Jonathan, then walked up to a long, curved wooden counter.

"We'd like to see the . . . the library director," she said to a round-faced young man behind the desk. He backed up and glanced into the doorway of a small office.

"She's meeting with someone right now. Can I help you with anything?"

Mrs. Pollack spoke up. "Sorry, but I think we do need to talk with the director. We'll just wait until she's done."

Keeping their eyes on the office door, the three stood fidgeting in front of a display of new books. "I'll be in the magazine section," whispered Mrs. Pollack finally. "Come get me when you need me."

As Mrs. Pollack walked away, Jonathan rubbed his hands together gleefully and turned toward one of the computers. Elizabeth managed to snag the back loop of his jeans. "Jon, you are *not* going to look for *The Encyclopedia of the Totally Disgusting*." Before he had time to argue, the two were approached by a slender black woman with close-cropped graying hair.

"I'm Josephine Taylor, the library director. What can I do for you?"

"We . . . uh . . ." Elizabeth hadn't thought about what to say. Jonathan, as usual, was tending to his shoelaces. "We're helping someone, and we need to find out what happened to his books. They were donated to the library a while ago. Well . . . two years ago."

"Two years ago? I'm afraid I can't tell you much about that. You see, we get several thousand books every year. Of course, we sell most of them."

Elizabeth could almost feel the word *stupid* blinking across her forehead. How could she think the library kept track of all the books people donated? "The books were from the Obermeyers," she said.

As usual, the Obermeyer name worked its magic. The director smiled. "Oh, yes. That was a wonderful donation. As I remember, Mr. Obermeyer's father collected mystery novels. He had some valuable old editions. In fact, many of those books are in our special collection."

She led them into a small carpeted reading room lit by a long stained glass window. The books lining the walls were not the colorful books Elizabeth was used to, but thick, serious books in dark-colored leather.

"Now this book, for example, is from Mr. Obermeyer's collection." Mrs. Taylor pulled out a book and set it on a round, wooden table. "One of the finest old mysteries. *The Moonstone* by

Wilkie Collins."

Elizabeth could almost feel her heart beating in her fingertips as she touched the smooth brown leather. "You see, we're looking for something," she said. "Something Uncle Rudy, I mean, Mr. Obermeyer thinks might be hidden in one of the books. He asked us to help him look."

"Well, normally we don't keep records of the books that are donated. The Obermeyer donation was quite valuable, though, so we did keep a list. I can get it, but if you don't mind, I'd like to call Mr. Obermeyer. Make sure he doesn't mind if I show it to you." She walked out of the room.

Jonathan threw his arms up. "Yes!" He danced around the room once, then descended on the book lying on the table.

"Be careful, Jon. It's really old." The two took turns gently flipping the pages and examining the binding. They found no sign of a coin or a key.

Jonathan paced around the table. "She said there are more of Uncle Rudy's books in here." He stood in front of the bookcase and began running his fingers down the spine of each book. Elizabeth did the same, hoping to find the telltale bump of a hidden coin.

"Hey!" A deep, accusing voice startled them from behind. Elizabeth jerked her hand away from the books and whirled around. The gruffness of the voice—like marbles rolling across sandpaper—made her think of Pop. But the man glaring at them was a stranger, an old man with a ferocious gray beard and a thick coat buttoned up to the top.

"Uh, we were just —" Elizabeth felt a sharp jab from Jonathan's elbow.

"Dusty," he announced in a loud voice.

Elizabeth stared at him, open-mouthed. "What?"

"Dusty," repeated Jonathan sharply. With the sleeve of his sweatshirt up over his hand, he began carefully wiping the spine of each book. Elizabeth turned around slowly. "Dusty," she repeated solemnly. "Very dusty." When she peeked behind her a moment later, the man was gone.

Elizabeth pulled Jonathan away from the books and sat him down at the round table. "All right. Just sit there and don't get any more bright ideas."

A few minutes later, the director reappeared. "Mr. Obermeyer told me you two are expert detectives. He asked me to help you in any way I can." She set three sheets of paper on the table. "Here's the list of all the books that were donated." She turned to leave. "Just let me know if you need anything else."

Elizabeth took page one. "Oh, great. There must be . . ." Elizabeth lowered her voice. The bearded man had come in again and was sitting in an armchair, keeping an eye on them. "There must be a million books on here," she whispered.

She ran her finger down the list. How would they ever find them all?

On item number twenty-seven, her finger stopped. Elizabeth stared for a moment, then gave a whoop worthy of the Outer Mongolian Warrior Dance.

"I found it," she yelled. She danced around the table, shaking the paper in the air. "Jonathan! It's not a key! It's not a key!"

Elizabeth saw the old man slip out of the room. She didn't care if he was going to report them. She didn't care about anything except three small words typed on the page.

"Quit being weird, Elizabeth. You're gonna get us in trouble. And what are you yelling about?"

Elizabeth slapped the paper onto the table. "It's so simple, Jon. But we never thought of it. We've been looking all over for a key. But the hidden key . . . " She tapped her finger on the paper. "The hidden key isn't a key at all. It's the title of a *book*."

A Puzzling Clue

"A book?" Jonathan sat back, his mouth gaping open like a choirboy holding a high note. The clue they were looking for was right in front of them. *The Hidden Key*, by Wendell Prescott. Elizabeth read the words four times, afraid they would disappear if she took her eyes off the page. Jonathan sprang into action, nearly knocking down the chair in his hurry to get up. He began desperately combing the shelves for the book. "You have to look over here, Jonathan," said Elizabeth. "It would be where the *P*s are. For *Prescott*."

After quickly scanning the titles, Elizabeth rushed out of the room. "It's not here. We have to look in the computer. And don't get Mom yet. We'll surprise her."

Elizabeth rushed over to a group of four computers lined up near the book check-out. Jonathan hopped up and down, warming up for his victory dance. Elizabeth pressed the key to start a title search. Carefully, she typed in *The Hidden Key*.

"Well, here goes." As Elizabeth pressed the return key, the screen went blank for a moment, then a list of titles rolled onto the screen. She and Jonathan leaned forward and focused on a title highlighted in green. *Closest title found: The Hidden Staircase*. Elizabeth looked at the top of the screen and read the computer's message. *You searched for the title The Hidden Key. Your title is not found.* Elizabeth stared at the last five words. *Your title is not found.*

"Wait. This can't be right." She typed the title again, this time without the word *The*. The message was exactly the same. *Your title is not found.* Elizabeth tried searching for the author, but the computer found no book by an author named Wendell Prescott.

Mrs. Taylor walked up from behind. "Need some help?"

"I'll say we do," said Elizabeth. "We know exactly the book we need to find. It's called *The Hidden Key*, and it's the main clue, and . . . oh, it's pretty complicated." Her voice sank to a whisper. The old man from the reading room had reappeared and planted himself in front of a computer. He wasn't typing anything, just standing. And listening.

"It's right here on the list," continued Jonathan. He handed the paper to Mrs. Taylor. "We have to find that book. But it's not in the computer."

Mrs. Taylor looked at the paper. "I don't think you'll like what I have to tell you. You see, we didn't keep all the books the Obermeyers donated. If this book isn't in the computer, I'm afraid it's been—"

"Sold?" Elizabeth could barely say the word.

"We have a used book sale every year on Valentine's Day to raise money for the library. So that means the book you're looking for would have been sold a little over a year ago."

"But we have to find out where it is," said Jonathan. "A year isn't that long ago."

Mrs. Taylor shook her head. "I can't think of how we could trace it. There are hundreds of people who come to the book sale. And the books that aren't sold are taken to a company to be recycled."

Elizabeth groaned. She could picture their only clue dissolving in a giant vat of paper pulp. "Could we move over here?" She slid back a few steps. The old man was leaning over, nearly bent in half in his effort to eavesdrop. Elizabeth eyed his long beard suspiciously. It could be fake. Some kind of disguise.

Suddenly, the man walked toward her. Elizabeth drew back, but as he brushed past her, he thrust a piece of paper into her hand.

More curious than afraid, she looked at the note, then handed it to Jonathan.

"I don't get it," he said. "It just says *Mostly Mysteries*." He held it up for Mrs. Taylor.

"Interesting," she said. "Definitely worth a try. Let me get you something." She took them behind the wooden counter and pulled out a thick telephone book. "Mostly Mysteries is a small book shop that sells used books. Mostly mysteries, just like the name says. Every year the owner comes to our book sale. He does buy quite a few of our mysteries. There's a chance he bought the book you're looking for."

Elizabeth saw the old man shuffling out the wide double doors of the library. She could see now why he walked so slowly. His battered black shoes had no laces.

"Do you know that man?" she asked.

"Well, he's a bit of a mystery himself," said Mrs. Taylor. "I don't know much about him, but he spends quite a bit of time here, especially when the weather's cold."

"Do you think he's homeless?" asked Jonathan.

"Oh, yes. He's homeless. In the winter he sleeps at the shelter down the street and comes here almost every day. He doesn't say much, just reads newspapers and watches what's going on. That's why he could help you. He knows everything about the library."

Mrs. Taylor opened a telephone book. "If I were you, I'd follow up on his tip. I'll write down the address and some directions."

Elizabeth and Jonathan found their mother in a large reading room, sitting in an armchair and chuckling over a novel.

"Oh, sorry," said Mrs. Pollack. "I was going to check and see if you needed any help, but I got involved in a book. Blame it on P.G. Wodehouse." She closed the book. "So did you find anything?"

"We found the hidden key," said Jonathan, pulling his mother out of the chair. "Well, sort of."

"There's this bookstore we have to go to," said Elizabeth. "Right now. We'll tell you all about it on the way." The two dragged their mother back to the hotel and went straight to the parking garage. "We've got the address and Mrs. Taylor even drew a little map."

Jonathan and Elizabeth kept an eye out for Mostly Mysteries while Mrs. Pollack drove down a long, busy street crowded with shops. Jonathan was the first to spot the bookstore. Mrs. Pollack edged the car over to the curb.

"Wait, don't get out," she said. "This is a no parking zone. I'll drive around the block and see if I can find a spot."

Jonathan already had one leg out the door. "That's okay, Mom. We'll go in first." Elizabeth jumped out and raced after him. The two stood in front of the store and looked up at the sign hanging over the window. Mostly Mysteries. From the bottom of the capital M, thick drops of red paint dripped like blood.

Through the window Elizabeth could see a maze of towering book cases, crammed full from top to bottom. A pale young man sat behind a cluttered desk near the door. Holding a book close to his face, he was nestled into an oddly narrow, high-backed chair. Jonathan was on his way in by the time Elizabeth realized what it was. The back of the chair was the top half of a coffin.

The young man welcomed them with a loud slurp from an oversized coffee mug. "Welcome to Mostly Mysteries," he drawled. "Milwaukee's largest selection of mystery and suspense novels. My name's Edwin and I'll be your server today." He swept a shock of coal black hair away from his eyes.

"Uh . . . yeah." Elizabeth tried not to stare at the two rings in his eyebrow or the small gold stud in his nose. She aimed her eyes at the middle of his forehead.

"We're looking for a book," she said. "*The Hidden Key*, by Wendell Prescott."

"Wendell Prescott," he repeated slowly. He eased out of the chair and slouched away, his baggy black pants scraping against the scuffed wooden floor. He disappeared into a narrow tunnel of bookcases. "Nope." He shook his head as he reappeared. "We don't have anything by Wendell Prescott. We do have some Nancy Drew

books though. Some nice old editions."

"But we don't need Nancy Drew," said Jonathan. "We just need a book called *The Hidden Key*. It's really important."

"Well, I suppose I could look at the bargain shelves upstairs. That's where we keep the books that don't sell as fast." He glanced toward the back of the store, to a dreary staircase covered with ragged scraps of carpet.

"We'll wait here," said Jonathan quickly. "Our mom is coming."

"Cool." The young man glided away, ducking his head as he went through the small doorway to the staircase. Elizabeth could hear the floorboards creaking overhead. Slow footsteps. A pause. More slow footsteps. Another pause. Elizabeth closed her eyes. She could feel her fingernails digging into the palms of her tightened fist. The footsteps quickened.

"What's up?" Mrs. Pollack swept through the door with a rush of cold air.

Elizabeth popped open her eyes. "We talked to the guy who works here and he thinks it might be . . ."

Suddenly the young man was in front of them, holding out a book. It was a thick book, with a dull orange cover the color of an old pencil eraser. He blew a puff of dust from the top of the book before handing it to Elizabeth.

"*The Hidden Key*, by Wendell Prescott." He bowed slightly.

"Wow, thanks!" Jonathan didn't have room for his Outer Mongolian Warrior Dance, but he managed to hop on one foot while turning in tight circles.

"Hey, you got the rhythm," said the young man. "Glad I could make you happy." He sat down and settled back as if he were watching a movie.

Slowly, Elizabeth opened the book. On the inside of the cover were two words penned in thick brown ink. The two most welcome words in the world. *Wilhelm Obermeyer.*

Elizabeth hugged the book like a long lost friend. "This is it. His name is in it." She spun around as Jonathan lunged for the book.

"Not *yet*, Jon." She turned toward the door, with Jonathan and Mrs. Pollack following. She squeezed the book tight, fearing that something might fall out and be lost.

"Uh, . . . guys? That'll be two dollars."

"Sorry!" Mrs. Pollack dug around in her purse and tossed a five dollar bill on the desk. "Thanks very much. And keep the change."

The book was kept in the front seat to prevent a battle, but Elizabeth was the first to inspect it when they were back in their hotel room. With the other two looking on, she set the book on the desk in the sitting room. She pushed up the sleeves of her sweatshirt and rubbed her fingertips together, like a master thief about to crack open a safe. She ran her finger down the spine of the book, but she could tell nothing was hidden there. She flipped through the pages, holding the book upside down. Nothing fell out.

"There must be some writing in here," she said, "telling where the coins are hidden." One by one, Elizabeth turned the pages until she had looked at all 342 pages. No message, not even a word in the margin. Jonathan and Mrs. Pollack had no better luck.

Elizabeth paced around the room. Why couldn't anything be easy with this case? It was like a trick someone played on her once, tying a thread to a dollar bill and pulling it away every time she bent to pick it up.

"I can only think of one thing," she sighed. "I've got to read the whole book. The clue must be in the story. Maybe someone in the book hid something, and Uncle Rudy's father did the same thing." Elizabeth propped up the pillows on her bed and settled down for a long read. *The Hidden Key* felt comfortable in her hands, with thick, soft pages aged to the color of an almond. After straightening her pillows one more time, she began to read. *Chapter 1. A Dangerous Voyage.*

"Well?" Jonathan pulled up a chair next to the bed and stared at her.

"Well what? I've only read two sentences." She turned toward the wall. "And I can't read with you staring at me. Why don't you go play cards with Mom or something?" After Jonathan went into the sitting room, Elizabeth raced through the first chapters, skimming over the words as fast as she could. 1923. A ship bound for France. Men with mysterious smiles and long foreign names. Rich ladies who fainted every time they heard bad news.

"We'll have to get ready soon," called Mrs. Pollack from the next room. "We're invited over to Uncle Rudy and Aunt Lorraine's house for dinner tonight. And later your dad's coming in on the train. If it's on time he might be here when we get back to the hotel."

"Yeah, okay." Elizabeth took off her glasses and rubbed her eyes. In chapter four a diamond necklace had been stolen—she could have predicted that. And one of the men, a count, found his long lost brother who had been separated from the family at birth. Elizabeth read on.

"That's strange," she said softly. She bent closer to the book, so close that she could smell the dusty dryness of the paper. Page sixty-seven. In the word *necklace,* the letter *a* was underlined lightly in pencil. Elizabeth stopped reading and slowly turned the pages. On page ninety-three the letter *t* in *captain* was underlined. Elizabeth slipped her hand into her backpack and pulled out her detective notebook and pen. She wrote down the two letters. By the time she found the third underlined letter, on page 122, she felt as if an army of ants were crawling up her spine. This was it. The message from Uncle Rudy's father was taking shape, letter by letter. She made her way through the book, hunting through the pages with slow sweeps of her hand. After finishing the last page, she slammed the book shut and rushed into the sitting room. Jonathan and Mrs. Pollack were sitting on the floor with a pile of cards between them.

"Ace Detective Elizabeth Pollack has just discovered the clue of *The Hidden Key,*" she announced. She dropped the notebook into Jonathan's lap. "Take a look at that."

"But . . . I don't get it." Jonathan stared at the letters on the page.

A T L U Y R I Z C Q

Finding the Answer

"All those letters were underlined," said Elizabeth. "It must be a message in code." She ran into the bedroom. "*How to Think Like a Detective*," she yelled. "*Chapter Eight. Cracking Codes.*"

Jonathan let out a low moan as Elizabeth pushed the book under his nose.

"Okay. One of the simplest codes is just to reverse the letters of the alphabet. Everything is backwards. So instead of *A*, you write *Z*, and instead of *B*, you write *Y*. Look, there's a chart."

Using the decoding chart, Elizabeth came up with the word *zgofbiraxj*. "Well," she admitted, "maybe that's not the right code."

"Could I make a suggestion?" asked Mrs. Pollack. "I know this may sound too simple, but what if it's just a word with the letters scrambled and not a code at all. There's a Q and U. Those would have to go together, and the next letter would have to be a vowel."

"I guess we could try," said Elizabeth. "Let's all work by ourselves." She came up with QUARCLITZY and CRITZYQUAL, then decided it might be more than one word. TRY CZ QUAIL. QUIZ AT CLYR. RITZY QUACL. She pushed her paper away. She had never been any good at word scrambles. "How did you do, Jon?"

"*Quazlcrity*," he said.

"*Cirly quatz*," added Mrs. Pollack. "Or *quit zyrcal*."

Elizabeth groaned. Her mind was beginning to feel like scrambled eggs. "Let's take a break, then give it one more try before we go." She flopped down on the bed and began leafing through a magazine. As soon as Mrs. Pollack went into the other bedroom to change her clothes, Jonathan disappeared into the bathroom.

Elizabeth sat up. A sweet, heavy scent of lilacs wafted through the air. Then something else. Cinnamon, maybe, with a little pine mixed in.

"Mom, Jonathan's fooling around with the aromatherapy again." Elizabeth ran to the bathroom door. It was locked. Of course. "Jonathan, you're making me sick, mixing all those smells."

"Pookie McDougal says you can use chemicals to make any smell in the whole world. Even dinosaur breath. Or a cesspool." There was a short silence. "What's a cesspool, Elizabeth?"

"I don't know, Jonathan. And I don't want to know. Just quit acting crazy."

Suddenly the door clicked open and Jonathan shot out into the bedroom. "Thanks for calling me crazy," he shouted. "Out of my way. I'm having a flash. Just like Uncle Rudy." He ran into the sitting room and bent over a piece of paper, scribbling something down on the page.

With a wild screech, he did two turns around the coffee table, then leaped into the air and caught an imaginary football. He ran into the bedroom, where he held up his hands and did a victory dance in the end zone. "You called me crazy," he shouted. "Crazy quilt! Crazy quilt!"

At first Elizabeth thought Jonathan had gone from weird to insane. But when she looked at the letters of the clue, she saw that he was right. The letters could be unscrambled to spell the words *crazy quilt*.

"But it doesn't mean anything, does it?"

Mrs. Pollack came out of the bedroom. "Actually, it does. I learned about that in my quilting class last fall. It's . . . Just let me think." She tapped her fingertips together. "Now I remember.

Crazy quilts were made with small pieces of material. They were sewn together every which way, with no particular pattern. I think they were often done in dark colors and —"

"Mom! I've seen one!" shouted Elizabeth. "A crazy quilt. Just like you said. That trunk in Uncle Rudy's apartment. He took out his grandmother's diary, and there was a pair of wedding shoes and a dark-colored quilt."

All at once, the case became clear. Wonderfully clear. Uncle Rudy's father was a tailor. In search of the perfect hiding place, he had sewn the ancient coins into the crazy quilt.

Half an hour later, as they rang the doorbell to Uncle Rudy's apartment, Elizabeth remembered that she hadn't even bothered to clean herself up. She tugged at her ponytail, which had migrated to the back of her ear. After Mrs. Dornan opened the door and took their coats, Jonathan burst into the living room. "Uncle Rudy . . . oh, sorry." Uncle Rudy wasn't in the room. A frail woman with wispy white hair sat in a wheelchair next to the couch.

"That's quite all right, young man," she said. "I've been looking forward to meeting the two brilliant detectives Rudy's been telling me about." She held out her hand as Elizabeth and Mrs. Pollack came into the room. "Don't worry," she laughed, "I won't break." Mrs. Pollack introduced them to Aunt Lorraine. Elizabeth shook her hand gently. The fingers had almost no weight, like a delicate seashell worn thin in the sun.

After a sharp knock on the door, Zina strode into the room. "What's up?" She put her hand on Jonathan's shoulder. "You look like you're going to burst wide open."

"We know where the . . . Ouch!" Jonathan hopped on one foot while rubbing the other, which had been stomped on by Elizabeth.

"Wait until everyone's here." Elizabeth hated telling good news too fast. It was like gobbling down a big piece of chocolate cake without tasting it.

"First of all," she said when Mrs. Dornan and Uncle Rudy came into the room, "we found this today. It belonged to your father."

She reached into her backpack and handed Uncle Rudy the book with the orange cover.

"*The Hidden Key*," read Uncle Rudy. Suddenly his eyes widened. "*The Hidden Key*! But . . . it's a book! The hidden key is book! I would have never thought of that." He turned to his wife. "Didn't I tell you they were sharp ones, Lorraine? Brilliant! Absolutely brilliant!"

"And there's more," said Elizabeth. "Your father underlined ten letters in the book. They were all scrambled up, but they spell out the place where we think the rainbow cup coins are hidden." She looked at her brother. "I guess Jonathan should tell you. He was the one who unscrambled the word."

"Crazy quilt!" Jonathan shot the words out like a canon ball. "Like the one in the trunk."

Uncle Rudy couldn't seem to stop shaking his head. "You mean my grandmother's quilt? I . . . I never thought to look. It's been folded up in the trunk. No one has touched it since my father died."

Zina disappeared briefly, then struggled into the room with the bulky quilt in her arms. With tables and chairs shoved aside, she unfolded the quilt, spreading it over the white rug like a rush of dark water.

They backed up and stood around the edges, staring at the odd beauty of the quilt. Patches of jewel-bright silk had been pieced together with delicate stitching. The shapes and sizes had no pattern, as if a rainbow lay shattered at their feet.

Elizabeth leaned closer. In the very center of the quilt was a square of black silk embroidered with a bouquet of tiny flowers. Three red roses were carefully stitched into the dark cloth.

"Three flowers," she muttered. Elizabeth's whisper swelled to a shout. "This is the garden of three! *Don't forget the hidden key. It leads to a garden of three.*"

"The quilt's not very thick," said Zina. "We should be able to feel the coins." She was already on her hands and knees. "But I don't feel anything behind the flowers. The coins must be somewhere else in the quilt."

"We'll have to search the whole thing," said Mrs. Pollack as she knelt down. "Let's each take a corner and start feeling in toward the middle."

Elizabeth and Jonathan joined Zina and Mrs. Pollack on the floor. They each began at a corner, pressing their fingers lightly into the fabric. Slowly, they each made their way toward the middle.

After their hands met in the center, they started the process over, each taking a different corner. When this method led to no discovery, they lined up and went straight across the quilt, feeling desperately for the coins. They turned the quilt over and repeated the entire process. Mrs. Dornan brought them a large flashlight. They shined the light through every patch, hoping to see the shadow of a coin. Finally Zina stood up.

"I hate to say this," she said, "but the coins aren't here. They're shaped like little cups. We would have felt them. And if someone had taken them out already, we would have noticed the stitching torn out."

Elizabeth still knelt on the floor. How could the coins not be there? She might as well believe that two and two don't equal four. "But we solved the mystery," she said. "I know we did."

Uncle Rudy stood up. "No problem. No problem at all. You never promised you would find the coins. You just said you'd give it a good try. And you did. A darn good try."

"Of course, we'd like you to stay in Milwaukee for a few more days," added Aunt Lorraine. "I understand your father's coming in tonight. Take a few days and see the sights. It'll be like a vacation."

Elizabeth stood up and faced the window. She could see her own blurred reflection staring back at her. "You all right, honey?" Elizabeth felt her mother's hand on her shoulder.

"Yeah. I'm okay."

During dinner, Jonathan kept his eyes on his plate and managed only one helping of mashed potatoes. Elizabeth was silent. Conversation flowed around her like a stream of jumbled words. All she could hear was her own inner voice. She went over the clues again. They had found *The Hidden Key*. The letters underlined in the book spelled the words *crazy quilt*. The three roses had to be the garden of three. Step by step, they had been led to the quilt. But the coins. Where were the coins?

Elizabeth knew what her father would say. Every unexpected event is a step toward a new answer. A better answer. Just like in science. If two and two didn't equal four, she would just have to find out why.

While they were waiting for dessert, Elizabeth excused herself and walked back into the living room. The quilt lay spread out across the long white sofa. Above it, beyond the dark windows, the nighttime city twinkled like a starry sky.

Maybe the quilt wasn't meant to hide the coins, thought Elizabeth. Maybe it was meant to give another clue. She sat cross-legged in the middle of the room, staring at the bright patches of silk, commanding them to give up their secret. It was no use. The trail of clues had led them to a dead end, unless . . . Elizabeth bent forward. Just underneath the sofa was a corner of white. She crawled over and picked up a small scrap of paper. Written on it were two words. *Father D.*

Elizabeth hurried back into the dining room and set the paper on the table between Uncle Rudy and Aunt Lorraine. "I just found this. It was on the floor under the couch."

Uncle Rudy looked at the paper. "I don't know where this came from. *Father D.* Must be a priest whose name begins with *D.* It's not anyone I know." Aunt Lorraine shook her head as well.

"Do you think maybe it was in the quilt?" asked Elizabeth. "And it fell out when Zina unfolded it?"

"Possible," said Uncle Rudy. "Very possible. You just go ahead and keep it. Your newest clue."

"Maybe tomorrow it'll make sense," said Elizabeth. "Right now, I think my brain just rolled over and went to sleep."

Elizabeth slumped into her chair, too tired to think about the clue. Jonathan showed no interest either. He sat up straight, swaying slightly, ready to doze off into his strawberry shortcake. Elizabeth was glad when Mrs. Pollack bundled Jonathan into his coat and drove them back to The Edwardian.

Elizabeth shuffled into the hotel with half-closed eyes. The lobby was like a pleasant dream, filled with gentle music and glowing from top to bottom in tones of gold. But, somehow, the place was different. Elizabeth forced her eyes open. Something didn't fit. Like a tuba in the violin section. Her gaze was drawn to a high-backed wing chair facing the fireplace. A haze of smoke rose from the chair, slowly snaking its way through the lobby. Mr. P stood behind the desk, wrinkling his nose and scowling slightly. The young woman with the fancy dog hurried by, holding a hanky in front of its nose. Elizabeth and Jonathan looked at each other. Cigar smoke. Tension in the air. It had to be . . .

They tiptoed up to the chair and peeked through the leaves of a large potted plant. "Pop! What are you doing here?" They spoke the words at the same time.

Pop sent forth another cloud of cigar smoke. "What kind of a greeting is that?"

He received two pecks on the cheek and a surprised hug from Mrs. Pollack.

"Sorry," said Elizabeth. "It's just that we didn't know you were coming. Did Dad bring you?"

"Hey, there he is!" Jonathan pointed to the elevator.

Mr. Pollack strode over and put his arms around their shoulders. "I see you found the surprise I brought. So how are my two detectives? Any hot leads?"

"Well, we thought . . . we were sure . . ." Elizabeth couldn't bring herself to say it. That they had figured everything out. And then failed completely. She held her breath, but she couldn't keep back the flood. She hid her face and burst into tears.

Mr. Pollack looked at his wife. "What did I say?"

Mrs. Pollack and Jonathan described the ups and downs of the last two days. "We went to Uncle Rudy's tonight," said Mrs. Pollack, "and we were sure the coins were hidden in the crazy quilt. It was so disappointing. They weren't there. And we have no idea why."

Mr. Pollack put his hand gently on Elizabeth's arm. "Sorry," he said. "I didn't realize."

"Well, I don't suppose anyone's interested in what I have to say," snorted Pop. Elizabeth, still sobbing slightly, looked over at her grandfather. Couldn't he at least pat her on the shoulder? Maybe say something comforting for a change?

Pop reached into his pocket and produced two cassette tapes. "There," he announced. "That's what your old grandpappy's been up to."

"Uh, you made music tapes?" asked Jonathan.

"Music tapes!" Pop had to snort again. "I've been working on the mystery, of course. You remember Mr. Kruger, the man who translated the diary. Well, he and his wife aren't mad at me anymore." Pop straightened up and lifted his chin. "Now that they know me better, they've discovered how charming I am."

Pop didn't give anyone a chance to disagree. "We've been working on a project together. He's been translating Johanna Obermeyer's diary. Not just that one page. The whole thing. It's all on these tapes. That's why I came up here with your father. To give them to Rudy."

"Oh, that's good." Elizabeth couldn't work up much enthusiasm.

Pop sat back like a king surveying his lowly subjects. He took another long puff on his cigar. "You didn't find the coins tonight," he said, "even though every piece of evidence told you that you would. And I know why."

Elizabeth stared at her grandfather. "You know why?"

"The answer is here in the old diary." Pop paused dramatically. "You didn't find the coins for one simple reason. You looked in the wrong quilt. Johanna Obermeyer wrote in her diary that she made two crazy quilts. Almost identical." Pop leaned forward. "You find that other quilt and you'll find the coins."

A Long Shot

"It shouldn't be too hard to find a big old quilt." The next morning Jonathan had just made his third trip to the breakfast bar in the hotel restaurant. As always, he was optimistic when he had a plate of food in front of him.

Elizabeth was back in the room and on the telephone at the stroke of nine. She made two calls, and she wasn't surprised by the news.

"Pop's lead isn't going to do us much good," said Elizabeth. "I talked to Uncle Rudy and Zina. No one knows anything about another quilt."

Mrs. Pollack walked over to Elizabeth. "Look, honey, I don't know about you, but I can't even think straight about this case any more. Let's just take the day off today. Do some sightseeing and forget about the mystery for awhile. All we have to do is drop Pop off at Rudy and Lorraine's, then we can be on our way."

"Your mother's right," said Mr. Pollack. "You need to freshen up your brain cells." He handed Elizabeth a copy of the *Milwaukee Regional Guide*. "Here, why don't you each pick out one thing you want to do."

It didn't take long for Jonathan to choose the Discovery World Museum. Elizabeth leafed through the book. The Milwaukee Public Museum invited her to hear the thunderous roar of a life-size Tyrannosaurus rex. At the zoo they could see the lowland gorillas, or plants from around the world at the Conservatory. Elizabeth turned the page. She wasn't in the mood for anything.

She ran her finger down the list of March events. Arts Festival. No. Sport Show. No. Elizabeth sat up straight. Wednesday, March 10. Quilters' Guild Annual Quilt Show. Local quilts on display.

"I found something," she announced. "It's a . . . well, it's a quilt exhibit."

"I thought we were forgetting about the mystery for today," said Mrs. Pollack.

"But you said I could pick out anything I wanted." Elizabeth had no intention of changing her mind, so the others reluctantly agreed. Since the exhibit hall was close to their hotel, it was their first stop after dropping off Pop.

The family mixed with a small group of people trickling into a long, one story building. The large activity hall was a glory of quilts. They covered walls and tables, hung from the ceiling, and filled a stage at the end of the room. Elizabeth spun around. Every color in the universe must be here. Bright reds and buttery yellows. Electric blues. Cozy little pastel prints.

"Isn't this beautiful, Jonathan?" Elizabeth turned around. "Jonathan?" She trotted behind him as he headed toward the snack room. "Just a minute. We need to have a family conference. As long as we're here I thought we could just—"

"I know," said Mrs. Pollack. "You thought we could see if there's another crazy quilt like the one Uncle Rudy has."

"Well," said Elizabeth, "that was kind of the idea."

"All right," said Mr. Pollack. "I say we should give it a try. Let's split up. We'll all look around and see if we can find the missing crazy quilt." He pointed up to a round clock above the doors. "And meet under this clock in 20 minutes. Of course, you know the chances of finding it here are very, very small."

"I know, Dad. Probably about a million to one."

Elizabeth wandered off through the maze of quilts. She liked the patchwork ones best, with their dizzy patterns of squares and triangles. Among the crisp new quilts, the few old ones were easy to spot, with their patches faded into soft, gentle colors. Elizabeth hurried through the large room, looking at everything on display, from patchwork pin cushions to king-sized quilts. But nowhere could she find the colorful jumble of a crazy quilt.

After fifteen minutes, she walked back to their meeting place and found Jonathan at the snack machine. Typical. He had probably been staring at potato chips the whole time.

"I didn't find the crazy quilt, Jon. And I bet you didn't even look, did you?"

Jonathan ignored the question. "Pookie McDougal says everybody eats bugs," he announced. Elizabeth stiffened. If she had her way the words *Pookie McDougal says* would be banned from the English language. " 'Cause everything we eat," continued Jonathan, "has bug parts in it. Only we don't know it. Except sometimes they're big. Like one time Pookie McDougal found maggots in his—" Elizabeth clapped her hand over Jonathan's mouth. "Inis whumpftles," he gurgled.

Elizabeth steered Jonathan away from the snack machine. At the far end of the hall, a group of white-haired ladies sat around a table-sized quilt stretched out on a frame. Their pale hands fluttered like butterflies, dipping up and down as they put tiny, quick stitches into the quilt.

Elizabeth stood silently next to a woman sitting at the narrow end of the quilt.

"We're using the quilting stitch to sew the three layers together," said the woman. She sewed as she spoke. "There's cloth on the top and bottom, and filling in the middle. It doesn't take so long when we all work together."

"That's nice," said Elizabeth. "But I was wondering . . . do you have any crazy quilts here?"

"Crazy quilts?" The woman looked up from her work. "No, I'm afraid not. People don't make crazy quilts anymore. But how did you young folks hear about them?"

"Well, it's kind of hard to explain," said Jonathan, "but there's a crazy quilt that was lost, and we need to find it."

"It was made with pieces of silk," added Elizabeth, "and it had three flowers embroidered on it. Three red roses."

The woman stopped sewing for a moment. "No, I've never seen a quilt like that. How about you girls?" She looked at the other elderly ladies, but they shook their heads and continued their work.

"Well, thanks anyway. Come on, Jon. Let's go find Mom and Dad." As Elizabeth made her way through the crowd, she felt a light tap on her shoulder.

"Hold on there, Missy. Now that I think of it, maybe I can help you after all." Elizabeth saw a tiny woman with a halo of fluffy white hair. Her dim blue eyes floated behind spectacles as thick as a magnifying glass. "Years ago, I did see a crazy quilt like the one you described. It belonged to two sisters, Elsie and Emily Kohler. They lived together all their lives. Never married."

"Do you think we could go see them?" asked Jonathan.

"Well, now that's going to be a problem," said the woman. "You see, Elsie died about five years ago, and Emily took it hard. Real hard. She almost never leaves the house anymore. Doesn't see anyone. I don't think she'd let you in."

"But we have to see her," said Elizabeth. "We just have to."

"Well, how about this? I'll tell you where to find her, and you can try your luck. Now you just listen carefully. Emily Kohler lives on Vine Street, across from Veterans' Park. You can't miss the house. It's a big old Victorian on a corner lot, and it looks empty. Spooky, you might say."

Elizabeth pulled her notebook out of her backpack. After scribbling down the directions, she headed for a phone booth in the lobby. "We've got to call Zina. What if Emily Kohler does have the quilt? We can't just walk in and say we want to search her crazy quilt. We need to be with someone from Uncle Rudy's family."

"But what about Mom and Dad?" asked Jonathan. "They might

not . . ." But Elizabeth had already reached Zina and was making arrangements for her to pick them up in ten minutes. "Don't worry. I'll tell Mom and Dad. They won't mind."

Elizabeth and Jonathan found their parents admiring a collection of doll quilts. "You know," said Elizabeth, "you two should be spending more time alone together. Without us kids."

"Yeah. Get to know each other better," said Jonathan.

Mr. Pollack raised his eyebrows. "Which means that you two are up to something."

Elizabeth explained that they were going somewhere with Zina. She didn't give any details.

"Well, I suppose it's all right," said Mrs. Pollack. "As long as you're with Zina. But remember. We're all meeting at Uncle Rudy's apartment for lunch. Twelve o'clock sharp."

Jonathan and Elizabeth hurried outside and waited for Zina. It wasn't long before they spotted a small car, fire engine red. Zina pulled up to the curb and opened the door for them. "Ready for adventure! Where to?"

Zina checked her map briefly and headed toward Vine Street. As they neared Veterans' Park, she slowed down. Jonathan and Elizabeth scanned the houses. Most were simple wooden duplexes, lined up in neat rows like houses on a Monopoly board.

"That's it! That's got to be it!" Elizabeth pointed to a huge old house, which sat among the smaller houses like a crow in a flock of sparrows. After Zina pulled over, they stood on the sidewalk in front of the house. It was an immense and gloomy Victorian, with a round tower built into one side. Not a whisper of life stirred about the place. Heavy drapes closed off the windows, and a ragged army of overgrown bushes and weeds had taken over the yard.

"Better not go in there." A young boy appeared, slowly pedaling a bike with rickety training wheels. He spoke quickly, glancing nervously at the house as he spoke. "It's haunted," he said in a low voice. He pointed to a second floor window with faded green curtains. "The tower room. That's *her* bedroom. The lady that died.

But they never took her out of the room. I've seen her face looking out the window. And my brother saw it too." He tilted his face briefly toward the house then teetered away on his bike.

"Yeah, right," said Jonathan. "Like I really believe in ghosts." He opened a heavy wrought iron gate and led the way up a weedy brick walkway. After reaching the front door, Zina stepped forward and produced two ponderous bangs with an ancient door knocker. The sound withered away into silence.

Jonathan, standing by a large window next to the door, suddenly jumped to the side. The curtain covering the window had parted. A gnarled hand showed itself from behind and fluttered against the window like an angry bird. The message was unmistakable. Miss Emily Kohler had heard their knock . . . and she was telling them to go away.

The Tower Room

After a few moments the hand stopped its frantic dance, then slowly withdrew. The curtain fell closed. The house became still, as if it were holding its breath, waiting for the intruders to leave.

"Now what?" whispered Jonathan. "She'll never let us in."

"There might be one way," said Elizabeth. She slid off her backpack and pulled out a notebook and marker. "I don't know why she would have your grandfather's quilt, Zina, but if she does have it, maybe she knew him."

Elizabeth tore out a piece of paper and wrote on it in large, thick letters. She stepped back, sure that Miss Kohler was watching them. She held up the sign. THIS IS WILHELM OBERMEYER'S GRANDDAUGHTER. WE NEED YOUR HELP.

The three stood still as statues. Finally, the snap of an opening lock announced a decision. The wooden door opened just wide enough for one suspicious eye.

"What do you want?" The voice was strong, but low and hoarse. It was the voice of someone who hadn't spoken for a long time.

Zina leaned toward the door and spoke slowly. Something belonging to her grandfather had been lost, she explained, and it was very important that they find it. The door opened another two inches, throwing a shaft of daylight onto a wide face mapped with delicate wrinkles.

"I did know your grandfather," she said. "But not well. We went to the same church years ago. I don't think I can help you." She stepped back, as if she were about to close the door.

"It's a very long story," said Elizabeth desperately. "And it has to do with an old patchwork quilt. A crazy quilt made from pieces of silk." Miss Kohler hesitated for a moment, then slowly motioned for them to come in.

They stepped out of the sunlight into a dim entry hall. Miss Kohler stood in front of a wide stairway, silently inspecting them. She was a stern, towering woman, with dark gray hair pulled back tightly from her face. Her dress, in serious brown wool, gave her a distant, long-ago look, as if she had stepped out of the yellowed pages of an old magazine.

She led them into a parlor crowded with heavy furniture, then nodded her head toward a long velvet sofa. Elizabeth sat between Zina and Jonathan, hugging the backpack on her lap. She didn't like this room. The closed curtains kept it in a kind of strange, sad twilight.

"I don't go out of the house, you know." Miss Kohler sat on the edge of a chair, staring at her folded hands as she spoke. "But that doesn't mean I'm lonely. My family has lived in this house for three generations. Their spirits are all around me. And I have my books too." She gazed up at the far wall of the room, solid with books from floor to ceiling. "And now," she commanded, turning to Elizabeth, "I think you have a story to tell me."

Elizabeth began, letting Jonathan and Zina fill in details. They went over every step. The missing coins. *The Hidden Key.* The trail of clues that led to the patchwork quilt.

"We didn't find the coins in Uncle Rudy's quilt, so we were just about to give up," explained Elizabeth. "Then we found out there was a second quilt, just like the first. It was made out of pieces of silk. And there were flowers stitched into the quilt. Three red roses." Miss Kohler's eyebrows lifted slightly.

"We talked to a lady at a quilt show," added Jonathan. "She said you and your sister had a quilt like that. We were wondering if . . . well, if we could look at it."

Miss Kohler said nothing. She sat still, looking up at her books. Suddenly she unclasped her hands.

"This is just like a story, now, isn't it? And I do love stories." She pointed her finger at Jonathan. "You go upstairs with your sister, young man. Second door on the left. There's a blanket chest in there. I think you'll find what you're looking for. You may bring the quilt down here."

Elizabeth hesitated. "Maybe Zina could . . ."

"Now, I don't want a lot of people poking around up there. You two go on up. Zina will stay down here. With me." Her tone left no room for argument. They certainly didn't want her to change her mind.

Jonathan and Elizabeth were halfway up the stairs when Miss Kohler's voice called to them. "It's my sister's bedroom. The tower room with the green curtains."

Elizabeth just managed to snare Jonathan's arm as he tried to run back down the stairs. "That's the ghost room," he hissed, trying to shake himself free. "I'm not going in there. Forget it!"

Elizabeth held his arm in a tight clamp. "I thought you were the one with a heart that dared to face danger."

Elizabeth was able to convince Jonathan to continue, promising she would go first. Squeezing the railing in one hand, and Jonathan's arm in the other, she forced herself up the steep wooden stairs. She knew just how Jonathan felt. It was easy not to believe in ghosts out there in the sunlight. But here inside the dark old house, it seemed as if anything could happen.

They stood for a moment before the door to the tower room. Elizabeth had barely touched the white porcelain knob, when the door swung open noiselessly. Like the rest of the house, the tower room was dreary and still, cluttered with oversized furniture. Fairy tale furniture, thought Elizabeth, big enough to climb into and hide from a hungry giant. On one side of the room was a high dresser with deep drawers and a fancy mirror, and on the other a bulky wooden wardrobe for hanging clothes. At the end of a high bed was a long, dark chest. Long enough to be a . . . Elizabeth didn't want to think about it. She put her hand on the open door. She was brave enough to do anything as long as she had an escape route.

"You stand by the door, Jonathan. And *don't* let it shut." Jonathan looked back toward the stairway. "And if I turn around and see you're gone, I'll . . . I'll rip up your *Encyclopedia of the Totally Disgusting* and feed it to the pigs." Elizabeth wasn't sure if pigs ate paper, or even where she would find a pig, but the threat seemed to work. Jonathan stationed himself in the open doorway and Elizabeth took one cautious step forward.

She opened the chest slowly, feeling the weight of the heavy lid dig into her palms. Inside, a white sheet was tucked neatly over the contents of the chest. Elizabeth glanced behind her to make sure Jonathan hadn't deserted his post. With one hand still on the lid, she bent over and carefully lifted the corner of the sheet. Suddenly Elizabeth's hand began shaking so hard she was afraid the lid would fall shut. She didn't know how or why, but here, in this silent and ghostly room, was Johanna Obermeyer's missing crazy quilt.

Without a word, she scooped up the quilt, closed the lid, and rushed out of the room with Jonathan in the lead. As the bedroom door banged shut behind them, they clattered down the stairs and rushed into the parlor. Elizabeth dropped the crazy quilt onto a chair next to Miss Kohler.

Zina stood up. "It's just like the one my dad has! But how on earth could it have gotten here?" Miss Kohler put her hand on the quilt. She didn't seem ready to give it up.

"Now where *did* Elsie get this quilt," she muttered. "It's not from our family. I know that."

Elizabeth sat on the sofa. The piece of paper in the quilt. She had almost forgotten about it. "Does the name *Father D* mean anything to you?" she asked.

Miss Kohler looked surprised. "Why yes, it does. That's what we used to call Father Duffin. He was a young assistant priest in the parish. Oh, years ago." She turned to Zina. "When your grandfather was alive."

Mrs. Kohler leaned back in her chair. "Now let's see. That must have been around the time the roof of the church leaked so badly. Cost a fortune to fix. Father Duffin helped raise money to . . ." Suddenly she stopped. "Elsie won this quilt in a church raffle," she announced. "Father Duffin organized it."

"Father Duffin. Father Duffin." Zina turned away from the others and stood with one hand on the mantel, staring into an empty fireplace. "Now I understand! After all these years, I understand." She whirled around. "A telephone message. I took a message when I was about ten years old. My grandfather was in the hospital, not long before he died, and the manager of the King's Home called. He said, *Father Duffin came to pick up the cover, and I let him into your grandfather's room.* I didn't understand what he meant. I probably didn't even tell my parents."

Zina looked at the others triumphantly, but Elizabeth could only return a blank stare. Father Duffin came to pick up the cover?

"The manager said *cover*," said Zina, "but he meant *quilt*. My grandfather must have offered to donate a quilt to the raffle. He put Father Duffin's name on it. On that piece of paper."

"But when Father Duffin came," said Elizabeth, "he took the wrong quilt by mistake. So the quilt that was raffled off —"

"Was the quilt where the coins were hidden," said Miss Kohler slowly. "The quilt my sister won." She ran her hand over the dark patches of silk. "This is your quilt," she said to Zina. "I want you to take it. A beautiful thing like this should stay in the family." She motioned for Zina to take the quilt. "But there's one thing I want you to do. You must look for those coins right this minute. I can't miss the end of the story."

Zina walked over to the window. "May I?" As Miss Kohler nodded, Zina pulled open the curtains. An ocean of sunshine poured in through the window, washing away the dreary tones of the room. The brownish carpet became a deep, rich red, and the gray sofa, a soft blue. The room was beautiful. Simply beautiful.

As the quilt was spread out on the carpet, Miss Kohler looked on, with her hands pressed together. Elizabeth knelt on the floor with Jonathan and Zina, sweeping her hands across the quilt. "I found something!" she shouted.

Zina took a small pocket knife out of her purse and carefully cut the fancy stitching around the patch. Elizabeth tipped up the quilt and held out her hand. This time she felt a cold, smooth piece of metal slip into her palm.

And in the sunlight she could see the unmistakable glint of gold.

A Final Surprise

Elizabeth held out her hand toward the others. In it was a small golden coin, round and rough-edged, with a simple design like the blades of a windmill. Elizabeth felt a strange power in the coin, as if a slender thread were connecting her to ancient times and faraway places. What other hands had held this coin? What did the people look like? What did they buy with it?

"I wish I knew more about the Celtic people," she whispered.

The other four coins were easily found. Zina's grandfather had carefully sewn an extra piece of silk over the places where he hid the coins. Jonathan found two coins, each with the head of a long-necked bird carved into it. Zina's two coins had mysterious swirled designs.

They sat in the parlor with the five coins lined up in the sun on a wooden table. Miss Kohler slowly climbed the stairs and came back with a small black velvet box. "You just put those coins in here and keep them safe," she said. "And then you must tell me everything again, from the beginning. About how you searched for the coins. This is the best of all my stories. The very best." Miss Kohler settled into a wide armchair and closed her eyes.

Elizabeth looked at Zina and Jonathan. She knew they were burning to tell Uncle Rudy the good news. But it was hard to leave. Miss Kohler was like a hungry person standing in front of a banquet table. The food she longed for was words and conversation. Elizabeth took a deep breath and started with the mystery letter behind the clock.

Just as she finished the story, a small gold clock on the mantel struck the hour. Twelve feather-light chimes floated through the air. Zina stood up quickly, as if a spell had been broken.

"I'm sorry," she said, "but we really do have to leave." She pressed a piece of paper into Miss Kohler's hands. "This is my name and telephone number. I want you to call me if you ever need anything. And I do want you to meet my mother and father."

Miss Kohler waved at them from the parlor window as they drove away. Elizabeth, holding the black velvet box in her hand, turned around one last time. Miss Kohler was gone, but the curtains were still open.

After a short drive, Zina pulled into the parking garage of her parents' building and handed the car keys to the attendant. She gathered up the crazy quilt and hurried after Jonathan and Elizabeth. As the three stepped onto the elevator, no one noticed a man in a blue parka watching them from behind a wide stone pillar. A few moments after the elevator doors closed, the man walked into the second elevator. Without hesitating, he pressed the button for the twenty-fifth floor.

Zina knocked briskly on the door to Apartment 2507. As Mrs. Dornan answered the door, Elizabeth held the velvet box tightly in her hand. She pictured Uncle Rudy's face when he opened the box and saw the five ancient . . .

It was at this moment she saw him. The man in the blue parka was behind them, already stepping through the door. It was too late to warn anyone. "A telephone," she thought desperately. "I've got to call the police." Clutching the box of coins, Elizabeth rushed past Mrs. Dornan and opened the door to the den. She barely had time to close the door behind her.

She stood still, wooden with fright. She could hear an angry deep voice. She couldn't hear the words, but she knew what he was saying. He wanted the coins. And this time it was real.

Elizabeth flinched at the sound of the front door slamming.

"Who in the world was that?" It was Zina's voice, closer now.

Uncle Rudy answered her. "That was Benjamin Barkley. Better known as Busybody Barkley. Of all the nerve! Hanging around the parking garage for three months. Writing down license numbers so he can make a chart of who uses the guest parking. Tells me I have too many guests using the parking spaces."

Elizabeth couldn't believe what she was hearing. The man in the blue parka, the man who had been spying on them, wasn't a coin thief after all? Just some busybody checking on the guest parking? She should have been relieved, but she had a giant-sized problem. Elizabeth hadn't stepped into the den. She had opened the wrong door and found herself in the coat closet, with a furry collar tickling her ear and the handle of the vacuum cleaner sticking in her back.

She heard Jonathan's voice. "Hey, where's Elizabeth anyway?"

"What's all this blasted racket about?" Great. Pop was there too.

A few moments later, Mrs. Dornan offered to hang up Jonathan's jacket. Elizabeth froze, awaiting her doom. After swinging open the closet door, Mrs. Dornan let loose a ferocious shriek.

"Hey, look!" shouted Jonathan. "It's the monster from the Black Lagoon." Elizabeth shuffled out miserably into the hallway.

Later, in the living room, she explained why she had mistaken Busybody Barkley for a coin thief. "See, I knew he was watching us, but I couldn't figure out why. I thought he might want to steal the coins. He could have seen your ad in the paper, and was watching us to see if we found them." She gave a sheepish shrug. "And the man I saw near Pop's house. I guess he was just someone in a blue parka."

"I don't know about that," said Aunt Lorraine. "Mr. Barkley does have a daughter who got married last year. And I believe she lives in Walworth. By some strange coincidence he may have actually been there that day. I would say you were being very observant."

Everyone looked up at the sound of a knock on the front door.

A few moments later Mr. and Mrs. Pollack walked into the living room.

Zina, thankfully, changed the subject immediately. "Well, I think that little mystery's been cleared up. And now that everyone's here, Elizabeth and Jonathan have something they want to show you, Dad."

Elizabeth handed Uncle Rudy the velvet box. "I think you lost these," she said.

He snapped open the lid. "What in thunder! The rainbow cup coins! But how on earth . . . ?" Uncle Rudy took the coins and picked them up one by one, as the others crowded around.

"It all started at the quilt show," said Elizabeth. She didn't mind telling the story again. She could tell it a thousand times.

"We're so proud of you two." Mr. Pollack scooped up Elizabeth and Jonathan into a double hug. Jonathan squirmed away before his mother could do the same.

"You're darn good detectives," said Pop. He puffed out his chest. "Of course you did have some help from your grandfather."

Jonathan stood up and bowed deeply. "Your humble servant thanks you."

Uncle Rudy picked up two cassette tapes from the table. "You know, I've been given two treasures today," he said. "First your grandfather surprises me with these tapes. He went to all the trouble to record Mr. Kruger translating my grandmother's diary. And now you bring me the family coins. I just don't know how . . ." Uncle Rudy turned his face toward the window. He raised one hand to his forehead and began to cry.

Zina walked over and patted him on the shoulder. Pop, who was getting teary eyed himself, took out his handkerchief and gave a mighty honk.

"Well!" said Zina. "I know how you can thank them, Dad. You can start off by sitting down and writing two nice fat reward checks for $500."

Uncle Rudy straightened up and walked over to his desk. "The reward. Of course. For those two sharp detectives."

Elizabeth took her check and looked over at Jonathan. She didn't even want to think about what he would buy. But Jonathan wasn't even smiling. His lower lip was quivering, the way it always did when he was about to cry.

"It's not fair," he said in a small voice. "About the money, I mean. There was this man in the library who helped us. He told us to go to that bookstore to look for *The Hidden Key*. He doesn't have a place to live and his shoes don't even fit. And we're getting all this money and staying in a fancy hotel." He stared silently at the floor.

"Now, Rudolf," said Aunt Lorraine. "I think there's something you could say that would make Jonathan feel better."

Uncle Rudy shifted in his chair and fingered his checkbook. Zina continued. "You see, Mom and I have been trying to convince Dad to agree to a . . . ," she gave her father a meaningful glance, "*sizable* donation to the building fund for a new homeless shelter. It's not just a building. They're going to have a staff there to help people get on their feet and find real housing."

All eyes turned to Uncle Rudy. He looked at his checkbook and sighed. "Oh, all right. All right. I'm sure I can manage some kind of donation. And we'll see if we can find that man. Maybe we can do something for him. No problem. No problem at all."

Jonathan led a noisy procession into the dining room after Mrs. Dornan announced that lunch was ready.

"We're going to contact the historical society," said Aunt Lorraine. "That old diary is like a time capsule. Johanna Obermeyer recorded all kinds of everyday things. How much things cost, what kind of home remedies were used when people were sick. There are even some old family recipes."

"You know, Pop, if you didn't have Mr. Kruger translate that diary," said Elizabeth, "we wouldn't have known about the second quilt." She looked at her mother. "I think I understand about being a memory keeper, Mom. You can't let too many things from the past just disappear, because you never know. You might need them later."

Uncle Rudy raised up his large glass of milk. "A toast to the Pollack Detective Agency and to a mystery well solved."

Elizabeth lifted her glass in response, congratulating herself on making her little brother into a halfway worthy assistant. She turned toward Jonathan, but he didn't seem to be listening. He stared dreamily at his tuna fish sandwich, his face lit with a radiant joy that chilled Elizabeth to the bone. She was always suspicious when Jonathan looked too happy.

"I want to go right to Jack's Joke Shop when we get home," he said. "And Elizabeth, wait 'til you see what I'm gonna buy." He smiled at her, displaying a slimy round slice of cucumber behind his lips.

Elizabeth was about to give him a wilting stare, but stopped. She hated to admit it, but a mystery without Jonathan would be a little dull, something like a taco without the hot sauce. And of course there would *have* to be another mystery. Elizabeth and Jonathan Pollack, ace detectives, were just getting started.

Becoming a Memory Keeper

Make your own time capsule

A time capsule is a way of capturing the present and saving it for the future, just like Johanna Obermeyer's diary in the story. A time capsule tells who you are and what it was like to live at a certain time in history. Maybe you will look at your time capsule ten, twenty, or fifty years from now. Maybe you will show it to children of a future generation who will be surprised at how much has changed.

To get started, find a sturdy box or other container. The suggestions here will help you think of things to put in the box. Use your own ideas, too!

Tell about who you are

Write down your name, age, and address. Include a picture or a drawing of yourself. Write about your daily life. What did you have for breakfast, lunch, and dinner today? How did you spend your time? What are you wearing today? What do you see when you look out your bedroom window? What is your favorite book? If you watch television, what is your favorite show? What's the farthest place you've been away from home? Describe an outdoor game you play with other children. Describe an indoor game you play with other children. Describe a game you play by yourself. Write down a poem or rhyme you know by heart. Write about the three most important things in your life.

Tell about the world around you

Talk to an adult or look through newspaper ads to find out what things cost. A gallon of milk. A loaf of bread. A pound of bananas. A candy bar. A pair of shoes. A subway or bus ride. A gallon of gas. A movie ticket. A comic book. A television set. A computer.

What can computers do that you think is pretty amazing?

Who is the president of the United States?

Name two events during your lifetime that you think will be in history books. How did those events make you feel?

Are there any recent scientific discoveries which you think will be discussed in history books?

Imagine the future

Medicine: When you are fifty, what new ways might doctors have to treat diseases?

Transportation: When you are fifty, how will people get from one place to another?

Energy: When you are fifty, what kind of energy do you think will power our cars and run our machines?

What do you look forward to when you think about life in the future?

What worries you when you think about life in the future?

Include objects in your time capsule

Stamps, coins, a section of newspaper, a favorite comic strip, a weekly news magazine, photographs, small toys, a sports card, favorite family recipes, a TV guide, an ad for high-tech equipment. Anything else you think might interest people in the future.